Bagby, George

12.95

"Guarenteed to Fade"

Guaranteed to Fade

GEORGE BAGBY

PUBLISHED FOR THE CRIME CLUB BY
DOUBLEDAY & COMPANY, INC.
GARDEN CITY, NEW YORK
1978

All of the characters in this book
are fictitious, and any resemblance
to actual persons, living or dead,
is purely coincidental.

Library of Congress Cataloging in Publication Data

Stein, Aaron Marc, 1906–
Guaranteed to fade.

I. Title.
PZ3.S819Gu [PS3569.T34]   813'.5'2
ISBN: 0-385-14499-7
Library of Congress Catalog Card Number 78-6360

For
Barbara Noble
with
the author's
love and gratitude.
He is indebted to her
for
the hat.

Guaranteed to Fade

I

If Dodo Baines had never read F. Scott Fitzgerald, she'd know nothing about living. Believing herself to be beautiful and damned, she thinks she has taken this side of paradise as her residence. Her actual habitations are several: the plush acres of a Manhattan penthouse, the big place in the Hamptons, what she calls her Arizona adobe, and de luxe hotels in all the de luxe places. Her mind, however, is always seated this side of paradise, although there are those who will tell you Dodo has no mind. I have known her these many years, and it is my considered opinion that she has a brain of sorts.

Dodo is loaded and Dodo is lazy. I know no one who can touch her record in either department. Rated in terms of the effect she has on my royalty statements, she would have to be called Bagby's No. 1 fan. She buys every book I publish and, since it is her habit to order everything in two-dozen lots, it has never entered her head that she might make an exception of her friend George's books. She sends them to people, and each time there is at least one new name on her list. She believes that for a man to be hooked on George Bagby for life it takes no more than one book. In her gift-book distribution she operates like a drug pusher: with each volume she expects to create another addict.

Maybe it works and maybe it doesn't, but I'm not the man to knock it. Although all the trouble started at a party she gave in my honor, I am taking none of the blame. I was just the guest of honor. I had no part in the arrangements. She did ask me for a list of people I would like her to invite and I provided one, but none of the people on my list were involved in what followed. She insisted that some of them hadn't been on her list either, but more about that later.

She threw the party on publication day of one of the books. She had planned on two guests of honor: myself (the author) and Inspector Schmidt (the subject). The book, like everything I write these days, was an account of one of Schmitty's brilliant murder investigations. The inspector is Chief of Homicide, N.Y.P.D.

But at least in part, Dodo didn't have her way. The inspector declined. Official duties would tie him up. Where another woman would have coaxed, Dodo couldn't be bothered. I told you she was lazy. She took the inspector's excuses without question and went on with her party.

"I just didn't want the dear man to feel left out," she told me. "He had to be asked, but it's just as well. I don't think he would have fitted in."

It was the first I'd ever had any indication that Dodo gave a thought to whether people might fit in or not. It seemed to me that her guest lists have always been odd assemblages, but this was the party at which at least some of the bedfellows were not nearly strange enough.

To me Schmitty voiced no regrets.

"I know these cocktail parties," he said. "You stand around forever with a glass in your hand and your shoes on your feet. It's like being busted back to patrolman, and I've been there. My feet can't take it any more."

I've already told you that Dodo is loaded. Her father was S.O.B. Thwait. Officially it was Samuel Oliver Blagden Thwait, but no one ever credited more than the initials. It was impossible to look at him and believe the Samuel Oliver Blagden. In case you don't know, old S.O.B. was railroads. There are many who'll tell you that the reason why railroads went broke was because S.O.B. diverted their assets into his own coffers. Economists may find other reasons as well, but nobody ever pretends that S.O.B. ever did anything that was good for the railroads or that he ever did anything that wasn't good for S.O.B. Thwait.

Dodo, his only child and sole heir, came into an income that she would never be able to spend, and if there was ever a way of spending money that Dodo didn't know about, it could only be because it was some practice that had become extinct before she was born, like financing the discovery of America.

Under the circumstances, Dodo did the most natural thing: she married Raleigh Baines. He was also an only child and sole heir. Maybe the thought was they would comfort each other in their solitude. The Baines money is old money. When money has been aged for as much as five or six generations and it has passed even once in the female line so that the ultimate heir doesn't bear the surname of the founding pirate, nobody remembers its original source. It's usually a safe bet, though, that any great fortune accumulated way back then was hauled in by practices that in a later day would have landed a man in the pokey. The Baines money, it's been said, didn't stack quite as tall as the Thwait pile, but give or take a million or two, it could hardly have been noticeable at their level.

They were married five years and the marriage was childless. He had polo ponies; she had parties. There have been cases in which children have knocked off the old man. At least one historian suggested that as a small boy the Emperor Caligula made that the first of his crimes, but death at the hands of an offspring is rare. I have no statistics on it, since death at the hooves of polo ponies is not in Inspector Schmidt's province, but that may be less rare. In any event, after five years in double harness with Dodo, Raleigh Baines, thrown by a polo pony, died of a broken neck. Polo ponies don't inherit. Dodo did.

But enough about money. In pockets other than your own it's dull stuff. Let's leave it that Dodo has it. I can't say that she works hard at spending it, because Dodo never works hard at anything. She just lets it flow out. Since the outflow can never reach the level of her income, it should perhaps not be said that Dodo is extravagant. The money comes, some of it goes, and Dodo grows richer and richer. I am bothering you with this only because it's important that you understand Dodo's party, and it is difficult to understand anything Dodo does unless you understand Dodo's financial situation.

Nobody gives more staggering parties and nobody puts less effort into them. She manages that simply: she substitutes money for effort. That can serve as a capsule description of the whole of Dodo's life. She has a secretary, and nobody can remember when she didn't have her. It has been said that S.O.B. gave her this secretary in the cradle, but that may be an exaggeration. To my knowledge, however, the secretary predated Dodo's marriage to

Raleigh Baines. The woman's name—you're not going to believe this—is Patience Grimm. You'll have to take my word for it. I didn't invent it. Writing demands credibility. I would never dare anything that pat. Maybe the name reflects prophecy, but it is more likely that she carries it as a curse, shaping her life and her career to conform to it.

Dodo calls her Paysh because Dodo won't extend herself to the utterance of two syllables. Me, for example, she calls Bag. There is no profit to be had out of George, no second syllable to drop off. But back to the secretary—she is patient and she is grim. She serves Dodo as mistress of the revels. Although she whips up great revels, she does them grimly. Guys on the President's staff will organize a summit conference and bring lighter hearts and a merrier spirit to the job.

In preparation for a party Dodo always retires. Sometimes she leaves town, but, at the least, she goes to a hotel. Patience brings in caterers, who take the penthouse over completely. They do the food and the drink and the flowers. They provide waiters, bartenders, and musicians. They also supply maids who, I've always suspected, are moonlighting nurses. They take care of coats and hats, but they also furnish first aid. The invitations are engraved and the caterer has people who write a beautiful hand. They address the envelopes. Maybe they have specialists who lick the stamps. Don't expect me to know all the details.

At her own parties Dodo is a guest. On occasion she has been the first to arrive, but more often not. Guests who find only Patience Grimm on hand to receive them aren't disturbed. They don't need Dodo. The Dom Perignon is there and the tubs filled with the great pearls of gold-tinted, pale, fresh caviar. The party gets started and there are always people who get started with it, so they never get around to noticing whether their hostess is there or not.

Dodo never fails to make it. She may be late, but she gets there. This time she was late, but not by much. I arrived about twenty minutes after what she had set as kick-off time. As I turned into Fifth Avenue, there was Dodo just about to be unloaded from the Rolls.

Spotting me, she was immediately upon me for her kiss. The kiss is part of her ritual: you find yourself enveloped in chiffon, perfume, and Dodo's hair, and confronted with Dodo's left cheek. You are expected to brush that cheek lightly with your lips. That does it. You have greeted Dodo in the manner to which she is accustomed.

"Bag," she said. "You're a louse. I've invited all these people to meet you and you're not there to be met. What'll they think?"

"They'll think I was delayed by having to stop to bring them their hostess."

"Me? Don't be sil. They're not coming for me. They're coming for you."

I could have told her they were coming for the champagne and the caviar, but Dodo may be the only one who thinks I have the world at my feet, and I wasn't about to disillusion her.

Other guests were arriving. We rode up to the penthouse in a well-filled elevator. Dodo was kept busy throughout the ride. She had to offer each and every one of them her left cheek. With the women the ritual was slightly different. They just touched left cheeks briefly as they wafted kisses into the air.

Up at the penthouse, we were no sooner disembarked from the elevator than a whirlwind came at us. Allegra Thomas pounced on Dodo. They touched the left cheeks but, even as they were touching, Allegra began telling Dodo off.

"You're the bitch of bitches, Dodo," she screamed.

"Of course, I am," Dodo said. "You know it and I know it, but, Al dear, must you tell the whole world?"

"I never thought you'd asked him," Allegra stormed.

"How could I not ask him? He's one of Bag's friends and, besides, I've known him forever. When our nannies wheeled us in the park, we used to spit at each other pram to pram."

There was no need for them to identify the man under discussion. It could have been none other than Tommy Thomas, the husband from whom the New York Supreme Court had only within the preceding months put Allegra asunder.

"If I had known," Allegra said, "I would never have come."

"You aren't compelled to stay, Al dear," Dodo told her.

"And give him the satisfaction of thinking he's driven me away? Not in a million years."

Dodo patted her arm.

"That's right, dear," she said. "After all, you'll be running into him all the time. You might as well get used to it."

She sailed off. The place was full of people who were waiting for Dodo's left cheek. Allegra watched her go.

"She is a bitch, you know." That was for me alone. She

dropped her voice to a whisper. "You know what she's done?"

"She's asked both you and Tommy to this do of hers. Ride with it, kid."

"She's asked all of us."

"All of whom?"

She'd lost me.

"Look around," she said. "We're all over the place."

"Who are 'we'?" I asked.

She ticked them off on her fingers.

"Louella," she said. "Agnes, Charlotte, Claire, and Constance."

It did seem excessive—Allegra Thomas, Louella Thomas, Agnes Thomas, Charlotte Thomas, Claire Thomas, and Constance Thomas. They weren't sisters, except possibly under the skin. Tommy Thomas was the marrying kind. One in that succession of wives—I think it was Claire, though it may have been Charlotte—was quoted as saying, after her divorce from Tommy, that to know Tommy Thomas was to love him, but to marry him was to hate him. Leaving aside the embittered epigrams, it was interesting to see them all together, the six women who had married Tommy Thomas. They had done it successively (it had never been a harem). They had all six of them married in haste, but there was never any leisure in their repentance. None of the marriages had lasted more than a year, but Allegra held the speed record. She had been in and out within a hundred days.

In appearance there was little resemblance among the six Mrs. Thomases, although they were all good-looking women, splendidly shaped. Tommy had always had an eye for the decorative. Otherwise they varied in height, in weight, in eye color, and in complexion tint. Hair color defied comparison, since all six were given to changing theirs at frequent intervals.

In character, in personality, and in mental set, however, they might have been Xerox copies. Six women could not have been more alike. What became obvious when one saw them together was that Tommy and his parade of wives had the misfortune of being people who were attracted to and attractive to precisely the kind of mate they could never live with. Tommy, of course, just went on making the same mistake over and over. None of his wives, however, had tried marriage again with anyone. They kept their relationships with men unofficial and unsanctified. It could be assumed that one go with Tommy Thomas was enough to cure a woman of any wish to reach once more for connubial bliss.

"Why not?" I said. "You should get along like a house afire. Aren't you a sextet with a lot in common?"

Allegra sniffed.

"If you call him a lot," she said.

"It's a big party and a big apartment. You can avoid him easily enough."

She was carrying a handbag that must have been the biggest number Vuitton ever turned out. She opened it and went fishing around in it.

"I'm not running away from him," she said, "and he better not get funny with me."

She started bringing stuff out of the great maw of the Vuitton. Until she got down to what she wanted, she kept handing me stuff to hold for her. First came her engraved invitation to come to Dodo's to meet George Bagby. Then there were her cigarettes and a lipstick. Those were followed by a pretty little pistol. Vuitton doesn't make them, so she couldn't have it with the redoubtable Louis' LV monogram, but she had managed to find one that went nicely with the bag. When she handed that to me, I looked it over carefully. It was fully loaded.

"Do you have a permit for this?" I asked.

"Permit for what?"

She was giving me scant attention. She was concentrated on locating and digging out whatever it was that she'd lost in the bag's vast interior.

"The Surgeon General says cigarettes are a hazard to your health," I told her, "but you don't need a permit to carry them."

Taking a moment out from her hunt, she glanced at the pistol.

"Oh, that," she said. "It's only a gun. I carry it in self-defense."

"No difference. You need a permit for it anyhow. You also need to have your head examined."

"That's what *you* think," she said. "Wait till I find the damn thing. I want you to read it."

"I make it a principle never to read other people's manuscripts," I said.

"It isn't a manuscript, it's a letter."

"I make it an even firmer principle not to read other people's mail."

"Anonymous letters aren't other people's mail. I have only one of them with me, if I can find it, but they're all more or less the same."

"You take anonymous letters to the police and they try to locate the sender. Guns you leave strictly alone. You know what's likely to happen if you try to use this?"

"Likely nothing," she scoffed. "I know what will happen. I'll shoot him dead."

"More likely he'll take it away from you and shoot you dead," I told her. "To people who carry guns and haven't had long training in handling them and using them it happens all the time."

"George dear," she said. "Have you forgotten where I grew up?"

"I've never known," I said. "You were all grown up before I first knew you. We didn't spit at each other pram to pram."

"Texas," she said. "About the time you were taking piano lessons or going to dancing school or something like that, I was learning to shoot. Want to see me get five of the crystal dangles off Dodo's Waterford chandelier with as many shots?"

"I'll take your word for it," I said.

She allowed herself a look of wistful longing cast in the direction of the chandelier, but she didn't reach for the pistol.

"Yes," she said. "I better not. I may need the bullets."

"For Tommy?"

"Who else?"

"You're rid of him. What's the beef now?"

"I'm looking for it," she said.

I waited while she rooted around some more and finally came up with an envelope. She retrieved from me all the stuff she'd had me holding, and dumped it back in the bag. The gun she left for last. When she took it from me, she held it for a moment or two while she looked speculatively at the chandelier's crystal pendants. Shaking her head, she returned it to the bag, and pushed the envelope

at me. I examined it. It was a plain envelope, the kind
they sell in boxes of a hundred at the five-and-dime. It
had been addressed to her and delivered in the mail. The
address was typed, and the typing had been done with
something less than professional skill. The sheet of paper
it contained did not match the envelope. It was of good,
solid stock, nothing fancy, just conspicuously good quality. The size was odd, just about square. It looked like
eight-and-a-half by eight-and-a-half. There was something peculiar about its lower edge—it didn't have the
precision-cut look of the other three.

The letter was also typed and showed the same flaws as
I'd seen on the envelope. It had been done by the same
inept hand. From the look of it, I could guess that it had
been done by the same inept two fingers. There was no
signature.

"Sure you want me to read this?" I asked.

"Sooner or later the whole world will be reading it,"
she said.

"If you're planning on publishing, let me warn you:
you never get all that much distribution."

"It will be evidence."

"Evidence of what? You already have your divorce."

"For when I've killed the man. I'll need the evidence
then."

"Just cause?" I asked.

"Self-defense," she said.

So I read the thing. It was so insane a document that it
was difficult to take it seriously, but threats are threats,
and even the crazy ones shouldn't be ignored. That's one
of the things I've learned in the course of my long association with Inspector Schmidt. In most cases, the writer of

poison-pen letters exhausts his venom in the act of writing, but you can't count on it. There might always be the odd one who will suit the action to the word. There might even be the guy who's forced to act simply because he's run out of paper.

There was no salutation, no preamble. It took off *in medias res.*

"Red pepper," it said. "Those hot, green chilies. Tabasco sauce. Has it ever occurred to you that you are a poisoner's dream? I can't imagine why I never thought of it. I had at least a million opportunities—all those Bloody Marys I made for you with never enough Tabasco in them. There isn't a poison you could have tasted past all that cayenne.

"It could even have been one of the corrosive things. You'd die horribly—your mouth and your throat burned out and your gut seared. It wouldn't, of course, be horrible for you. You wouldn't know what was happening to you. You'd just have thought that for once the fool hadn't been stingy with the pepper. It's something for you to think about now, though. Your next Bloody Mary, the next time you go to that Szechwan dump for another bowl of bean curd in hell-fire oil, maybe you'll be asking yourself the big question. Is it yummy or is it death?

"I'm still thinking. There are so many ways. It's just a matter of choosing the one that will be good enough. I haven't ruled any of them out. They're all still in the running. I'll be narrowing them down pretty soon, but don't expect me to let you know which ones I start eliminating. I was always such a bore, always so completely predictable. I'm a changed man, baby. Now I'm the guy you always wanted me to be, unaccountable, full of surprises.

That's why you can't know when it's coming or how. All you'll ever know is that it is coming. Maybe it will be in one of these ways, or maybe it'll be something completely different, a new way, one I've never mentioned. I can't say you'll never know, but you won't know for long—for no more than that last moment before you will be past knowing anything."

Although there was no signature, you couldn't quite call the thing anonymous. Its every word pointed to an ex-husband, and Tommy had been Allegra's one venture into marriage.

Having read it, I returned it to her.

"Well?" she said. "No comment?"

"Obviously he's trying to put you off your feed," I said.

"If he thinks I'm going to wait around until he tries something," she growled, "he can just think again."

"So what are you going to do about it apart from shooting him dead?" I asked.

"Apart from shooting him dead," she answered, "nothing."

"You've had a string of these letters?"

"One a day, like those vitamins."

"If you're smart, you'll take the letters to the police, and, while you're there, you'll turn the gun over to them."

"The police? Someone like that inspector friend of yours?"

"Inspector Schmidt could be interested."

"We Texans fight our own battles."

"You're not in Texas now. You're up here in civilized, law-abiding country."

"New York? You've got to be kidding."

"Just because we try to give the underprivileged a

break," I said, "don't you get any delusions. Nobody's going to call you underprivileged."

"I'm a woman."

"The operative phrase, Allegra, is 'poor, helpless woman.' You could never make it for the adjectives."

"You know what makes me maddest?" she said.

"What?"

"This is so unlike Tommy. If he had only been like this even once while we were married . . ."

"Then what?"

"We'd have fought it out and I wouldn't have been so bored. I wouldn't have needed to divorce him."

"Maybe he realizes that," I suggested. "This could be his second courtship."

"You're his friend?" she said.

"That's pitching it a little strong. I know him. I've known him a long time. I wouldn't say friend and I wouldn't say foe."

"You wouldn't want him killed."

"That's nothing—I wouldn't want anyone killed. I'm opposed to murder. I'm opposed to war. I'm opposed to capital punishment. And I'm opposed to Texan justice."

"Then you'd better talk to him."

"About what?"

"About me."

"You want me to talk to him?"

"Somebody has to do it. It's for his own good. Somebody has to warn him."

"And you've picked *me* to carry the message. Why me?"

"He'll listen to you."

"What makes you think that?"

"You're the only friend he has who knows anything about people killing people. You tell him that he's playing out of his league. He'll get himself hurt."

"Out of his league and in yours. Is that it?"

"Yes. That's exactly it. You tell him."

It didn't seem like a bad idea. I can't say it seemed so good or so pressing that I was about to leap into action. But sooner or later at that party, as groups formed and re-formed, I could have expected that I would come to-gether with Tommy Thomas. At such a time pistol-pack-ing Allegra could have been as good a topic of conversation as any. I was going to keep it in mind.

I never did get to talk to him. With time, the natural currents of the party would have separated me from Alle-gra, but Patience Grimm wasn't waiting for the action of any natural currents. She came barging up to detach me. She was at her grimmest.

To me she was only barely polite. To Allegra she was unmitigatedly rude.

"George," Patience said, "there are invited guests here who have not met you."

Need I tell you that Allegra wasn't the girl to let a crack like that pass?

"What does that make *me?*" she asked.

"Can it be you don't know?"

"Don't give me that," Allegra snapped. "You make up the list for Dodo. You know damn well you had me on it, me and all the others, and him too. How you must have laughed!"

"Mr. Thomas was on the list."

Allegra plunged into the Vuitton carry-all for another paw-through. I didn't really think she was going to come up with the pistol, but I wasn't playing it entirely for laughs. It didn't seem right that the Grimm should go unwarned.

"Watch it," I said. "She's armed."

"Don't be an idiot," Allegra mumbled.

She was not sparing me much attention. She was too much preoccupied with her search. She came up with what she wanted and she pushed it at us. For a moment I thought it was the threatening letter, but almost immediately I realized that this was a different one. Although the envelope was a different size and shape, and stiff and heavy, and obviously of better quality, in every other respect it looked the same. At a glance I couldn't know for sure that both had been typed on the same machine—to determine that would have required close and expert comparison—but it looked like the same dirty type and the same indications of mechanical deficiencies.

"So what do you call that?" Allegra growled.

Scowling, Patience took the thing from her hand. She pulled the card out of the envelope and subjected it to careful examination. I could see nothing about it that could warrant so much attention; I recognized it at a glance. It seemed to me that for Patience Grimm recognition should have been even quicker.

Hanging on to the card and the envelope, she fixed Allegra with a stern and inquisitorial eye.

"Where did you get this?" she asked.

No one should take that tone in asking a question without first having read the suspect her rights. If she had caught Allegra with one of Dodo's vermeil ashtrays stowed away in the Vuitton sack, both question and tone might have been suitable.

"Where do you think I got it? You sent it to me."

"It's obvious that I didn't," Patience said.

"It was addressed to me. It was mailed to me. It came to me in the mail."

"You were not on the list."

I made a try with what I thought was the obvious explanation.

"The people you had doing the addressing and mailing mixed up the lists," I said. "It happens."

"It doesn't happen to me," Patience said.

"Oh, come on," I said. "The kind of service we all get nowadays, it's a surprise when anything is done right."

"Our envelopes are hand-addressed," Patience said. "Look at this thing—typed and on an old machine with dirty keys. If it wasn't typed by some retarded child, it was done by someone who had never touched a typewriter before."

As she spoke she was looking pointedly at Allegra's beautifully manicured nails.

Mumbling imprecations, Allegra made another dive into her bag. This time I knew what she was after. It wasn't going to be the little gun. As I expected, she came up with the poison-pen letter.

"How's that for a son of a bitch?" she said.

II

Allegra wasn't waiting for the absolute verification of expert opinion. You may think she was going off half-cocked, but neither Patience nor I saw any reason to doubt her assumptions.

Patience seized on the second envelope. She was steaming. Someone had been playing games in her territory, and she was not the gal to put up with any of that nonsense. She was going to get to the bottom of this, and woe betide that bottom when she did get to it. I sloped off and left the two women to it. I didn't need another go-around on the crazy letter.

I did what was expected of me. I floated free through the party, behaving as a proper guest of honor should. I can't say I ran into many of those people who were supposed to be dying to meet me. Most of them appeared to be more than content with meeting the Beluga and the Dom Perignon, and why not? Both were at least as delightful as any of Dodo's guests and far more delightful than most of them. But Bagby was making himself available.

In the course of my drift I spotted a huddle that put a spur to my curiosity. A writer, after all, lives on people, and it is in the peculiar behavior of people that he finds his richest food. It was a group of five women, and you might say that they appeared to be as thick as thieves. I won't say it, because I've never made any sense of the phrase. I've known thieves in my time, and thickness has never been one of their attributes.

Louella, Agnes, Charlotte, Claire, and Constance. It was a convention of Thomases, lacking only its most recent member. They were so occupied among themselves and they looked so contented that I hesitated. I was thinking that they might not welcome an invasion, but they spotted me and they smiled and beckoned. Threading my way through the happy throng, I joined them.

"This is something," Charlotte said. "You've never seen the lot of us together before this. Nobody has."

"We've always been avoiding each other," Agnes added.

"And people have always worked at keeping us apart," said Louella.

"And now Dodo, bless her," Claire said. "I wonder what gave her the idea."

Only Constance said nothing. She was looking thoughtful.

"Allegra is here too," I said.

Constance looked even more thoughtful.

"A clean sweep," she murmured.

"What does she look like?" Claire asked. "I've never seen her."

"Me neither," Agnes said. "Is she nice?"

"We ought to go join her," Constance suggested. "Welcome her to the fold and all that sort of thing."

"Do you want to?" I said. "She's packing a gun and she says she's a crack shot."

"A gun," Claire giggled. "It would hardly be for us."

"What does she want with a gun?" Louella asked. "For who?"

"You mean for *whom*, dear," Constance told her.

"Who, whom, and why, and what for," Louella said.

"Tommy, and she's saying self-defense."

"That's silly," Agnes said. "After all, she didn't when there might have been some point to it."

"Maybe she didn't have a gun then," Claire suggested.

"When would that have been?" I asked.

"When he beat her."

"You think he did?"

"Of course, he did," Agnes told me. "What would make her any different from the rest of us?"

I looked to the others. I didn't feel like putting the direct question, but I didn't have to ask it. In unison they nodded. Constance amplified it.

"We've been talking about it and we couldn't have been in more perfect agreement. We just don't know which was the more infuriating—the black eye or the gift of Cover-Mark the next morning."

"Systematic wife beater," I muttered.

I was having difficulty matching up this item with anything else. It seemed too much unlike Tommy Thomas as I knew him. He had always seemed a limp and languid type. You can't black an eye without bringing to the job some measure of exertion, and it was difficult to imagine Tommy exerting himself that far. There was also Allegra. I'd had it from her own lips that it was boredom that had driven her to divorce. If even a threat of violence would have alleviated the boredom, how could she have been bored with the real thing?

I could think of only one possible answer to that. Of all

the Thomas marriages, his time with Allegra had been the briefest. It could have been that Allegra was different from all her predecessors, at least insofar as she was the impatient type. She wanted action and she hadn't waited around long enough for the action that would have come.

"Allegra," I said, "has been getting threatening letters. After you divorced him, did any of you ever get any?"

"Threatening letters from him?" Louella asked.

"From anybody," I said.

None of them answered immediately. They exchanged glances among themselves and then they all shook their heads.

"If she has been getting letters," Constance offered, "they haven't been from Tommy. He's never written a letter in his life. If you ask me, he can't write."

"Oh, come," I said. "Didn't he go to Yale?"

Agnes sniffed.

"What has that got to do with it?" she asked.

"Much good it ever did him," Claire added.

This turn the talk had taken reminded me of a time when Tommy Thomas had felt impelled to offer me some explanation of why he had never read any of my books. He'd explained that he'd taken the degree Yale awarded him as a lifelong license to refrain from reading. He hadn't mentioned writing, but it was not impossible that this license would have covered that as well.

"Telephone and tapes," Louella murmured.

The words struck a chord for the rest of them. They laughed. They were sharing a comic memory.

"You were the first," Constance said. "Even then, at the beginning?"

"I didn't mind," Louella told her. "It seemed fun, original, different."

"Yes," Claire said. "I rather liked that. It seemed more intimate than a letter, hearing it in his own voice."

"Hearing what?" I asked. "Threats?"

"Oh, no," Louella explained. "Endearments. It's always been his way of courting, no love letters, just interminable phone calls and the tapes—love tapes."

"They were nice," Agnes agreed. "Addressing the tapes for mailing, he always typed the address labels himself. He used this old, beat-up typewriter his father had given to him when he went away to school."

The girls were enjoying this looking back. Sentimentality was creeping in. Constance scotched it.

"You'd have thought with all the labels he'd typed by the time he got around to me, he might have learned to type decently."

That had the lot of them laughing again as they exchanged fond memories of jumped spaces and words run together, of caps that should have been lower case and the letters that hung somewhere between caps and lower case. They worked at filling me in, and what they were giving me was a perfect description of the two envelopes Allegra had displayed.

"Mind if I ask you who invited you to this do?" I asked.

The question startled them.

"Dodo," Louella said.

"Who else?" Agnes asked.

"After all, it is *her* party," Claire contributed.

"I suppose Patience does the guest list," Constance murmured.

She was thinking aloud and I had a hunch that she wasn't giving utterance to all that she was thinking.

"Patience insists that Allegra wasn't on the list," I offered.

"I can't speak for Allegra," Charlotte huffed, "but I can speak for myself. I'm no gate-crasher. I don't go where I'm not invited."

"I don't know about the rest of you," Constance said, "but I've begun having doubts. I don't think I was on the list either."

The rest of them looked at her with something like shock. In shared memories they had been building themselves a community of kindred spirits, and now they were wondering whether Constance could truly belong.

"You didn't have an invitation?" Agnes asked.

A look of anxiety was coming over all of them as they waited for the answer. Their looks were appealing to her. They were begging her to say it wasn't so.

"I had an invitation," Constance said, "but it was stupid of me not to have been suspicious of it."

"But why?"

They were asking pretty much in chorus.

"It was the usual engraved job Dodo always sends out," Constance said, "but the envelope was strange. It wasn't hand-addressed, and you know how correct Patience is about that sort of thing. I came close to throwing it away without opening it. I thought I recognized the typing, and I didn't particularly want to hear from him."

"Tommy?" Louella asked. "You can't mean Tommy."

"Crazy, isn't it?" Constance agreed. "But that's just whom I *do* mean. I thought about it and I decided that I really didn't mind, or maybe it was that I wanted to convince myself that nothing he might do or say could mean enough to me now for me to avoid it any more than I would invite it. Anyhow, I was curious. Then I found that it was Dodo's invitation."

"Sent to you by him?" Agnes asked.

Constance had thrown them into total confusion.

"That possibility just never occurred to me," Constance said.

"I should hope it wouldn't," Charlotte exclaimed. "You'd have to be out of your head to think that."

"What did you think?" I asked.

Constance was slow to answer. She was trying to recollect.

"I suppose," she said, "once I saw the invitation I didn't think at all. I thought perhaps Patience was slipping if she was allowing anything that sloppy to go out. It certainly couldn't occur to me that she had hired Tommy to do Dodo's addressing for her. I just thought that one piece of bad typing would look much like another and that I'd been letting my imagination run away with me."

"Allegra's invitation was just like yours," I said.

"I bet all of them were," Constance said, "all of ours."

"But the invitations?" Agnes wailed. "How would he have gotten hold of the invitations?"

I had an idea. I blurted it out as quickly as it came to me. Nothing could have been more simple or more obvious.

"Tommy was on the list," I said. "Dodo has known him just about always."

They concurred in that. Every last one of them had come to know Dodo only through Tommy.

"He had his invitation," I explained. "He takes it to

some printing and engraving shop and has it duplicated exactly. No trick to that. What he can't manage is the hand-written envelope. He manages the best he can. He types them."

Again they exchanged glances. In silent congress they shook their heads. They couldn't buy it.

"Tommy?" Constance said. "Where would he find the energy to go to so much trouble? And why?"

"Somebody else," Charlotte said. "Some idiot who plays practical jokes."

"Dodo herself or Patience," Claire suggested.

I tried casting Dodo and Patience in the role of practical jokers, but I couldn't make it fit. Dodo was too indolent, and Patience wasn't the type. When I said as much, I was confronted with another of their automatic agreements. They confronted me with everything that made it likely. Agnes tried to set me right on that point.

"Being a man," she said, "you may not know it, but there isn't a woman alive who won't on occasion turn bitchy."

Dodo and Patience had the invitations. It would have been almost no trouble at all for them to send them out, only the small job of typing those few envelopes.

"With the envelopes typed they could pretend they hadn't sent them."

"And Patience is a whiz typist," Louella added. "She could whip them out in nothing flat."

"Neatly and impeccably," I reminded them.

"If she'd ever seen Tommy's typing," Louella argued, "she could easily have imitated it. I can see where they thought it would make the joke funnier if we thought the invitations came from him."

"She'd have to find herself an ancient typewriter with dirty keys that were out of alignment," I objected.

"Oh, that." Constance found my objection trifling. She dismissed it. "You said you knew Dodo and Patience," she said.

"And?" I asked.

"Patience is dedicated. All it takes is Dodo's slightest whim and she whips into action. Patience is a wonder woman. She can do anything."

I couldn't dispute that. Nonetheless, I was not convinced.

"And Allegra's threatening letters?" I asked. "Would Patience have done them too?"

"Since it isn't Tommy," Claire said, "it has to be someone."

"If there *are* any threatening letters," Louella remarked.

I was about to say I could vouch for the existence of at least one, but the girls weren't listening. In a body, they turned on Louella.

"That, my dear, is bitchy," Claire told her.

"See?" Agnes said. "Any woman anytime, even one of us."

Weaving his way through the merry throng, Vernon Adams descended on us. He came bubbling with delight.

"Hello," he said. "Hello, hello, hello, and hello, not to speak of hello, George."

"You're going to need another hello, Vernon," Constance said. "George tells us Allegra is here too."

"And keeping to herself?" Adams said. "That's not like her. Where is she? I'll bring her over, or have the rest of

you met her? You must meet her. I'm sure that's what
Dodo intended."

"Do you know what Dodo intended?" Louella asked.

"She would hardly have asked all of you if she hadn't
wanted to bring you together, now, would she?"

"We have no idea what she would do," Constance told
him.

"Never mind," said Adams. "This is wonderful. It's like
old times."

"Your old buddy is here as well," Constance said.

"Tommy?" Adams was grinning. "He was here but
only long enough to see the lay of the land. He bolted.
The guy's chicken."

"Or perhaps he's acting on principle," Agnes suggested.
"I'll never forget the charming way he used to put it. He
wasn't a dog to return to his vomit."

Louella rose to that one.

"The reference, of course, would have been to me," she
said.

There was the beginning of a rift there, but Vernon
Adams jumped in with soothing words.

"No reason for any of you to take that personally," he
said. "The whole world knows that it was all of you
vomiting him. It's never been the other way around."

He'd found the right words, and with them he evoked
five smiles of smug contentment.

"I bought a hat the other day," Charlotte said. "It
reminded me of Tommy. It's just a cotton hat to go with
jeans—a gardening hat, you know. It has a label in it that
says 'Guaranteed to fade.' Could there ever be a better
description of marriage, or at least of marriage with
Tommy Thomas?"

Adams sighed.

"Poor Tommy," he said. "His gift is for friendship. It's been years and years and years, Tommy and me. They've all been good years too."

"We know," Constance said. "Nobody expects you to be disloyal, Vernon. You've never been married to him."

She was speaking for all of them. Adams appreciated it. He grinned.

"There was a time," he said, "when I could have told you I was the wrong sex, but things are not that simple any more. The options seem to be wider now, except that Tommy and I are too old for that sort of thing."

"Yes," Constance murmured, "and that's a pity. You might be what he's always needed. Anytime he gave you a black eye, you could have bloodied his nose. It might have been a healthier relationship than he could ever have had with any of us."

"You know," Adams said, "we've never had even so much as a quarrel in all the years."

It had been many years, I knew that. Certainly it was all of their adult lives, if not even longer. They were business partners, and it had always been the general feeling that it was the sort of partnership in which one member supplied the capital and the other all the business acumen. There could never have been any doubt about which would be which: Tommy Thomas had the money, and Vernon Adams had the business skills. Adams had all the drive that Tommy lacked. It was easy to understand how their relationship could have been uninterruptedly amiable down through the years. Adams had full command of the business and there was never any possibility of conflict. Tommy could never have worked up the energy or the interest it might have taken to question an Adams decision or to interfere in any way with his partner's management of things.

Since they were both free-spenders and they moved in circles of conspicuous affluence, it could be assumed that the business thrived. A wit had once remarked that Tommy's problems arose from his never having thought of delegating Vernon Adams to run his marriages for him.

"He should have provided the money and left it to Vernon to take his brides to bed," was the way it had been put.

What made the crack funny was the contrast in the looks of the two partners. Tommy Thomas was an anatomical phenomenon. He was a big and beautiful hunk of man who led the languid sort of life that should have turned him gross and flabby. He overate and he overdrank, and he conspicuously hated physical exercise, unless you count nipping in and out of marriage.

Nevertheless, year after indolent year he remained lean and muscular. He had always been the type you see in TV commercials where they appear as symbols of male vigor and rampant virility. The clear, healthy-looking skin, the wide span of shoulders, the broad expanse of well-muscled chest, the flat belly, the brawny arms, the narrow waist and hips, he had it all, and year after year he kept it while his contemporaries, despite dieting and exercise, were beginning to go pendulous along the jowls and protuberant in the middle. It was beyond understanding.

Vernon Adams, on the other hand, had always been skinny. Although the years had been putting weight on him, it was all undistributed weight. There had been no change in the pipestem arms and legs, and the scrawny neck had grown scrawnier—or perhaps it just seemed to in contrast to what now was a bulging belly and ballooning buttocks.

Another witticism that had long gone the rounds was that Vernon was fortunate that he had found Tommy to do his marrying for him. Tommy did enough of that for both of them. Be that as it may, Vernon had gone many years the confirmed bachelor, and the thought of Vernon Adams as a lover had been likely to throw any woman into paroxysms of laughter. This congress of Tommy's former wives was evidently most happy in Vernon's company. It might have been that he was just the right man for gals who had had all they would ever want of marriage.

I wondered a bit about his being at the party without his wife, since, just within the year, he had finally married and had become a slavishly devoted husband. I had met the lady on several occasions and had always wondered how Vernon Adams had managed to snare her. She was a lovely creature. Alongside her conspicuous shapeliness Adams looked more unshapely than ever.

It could hardly have been that he had won her with his looks, and it was obviously not his brain, since the lady— her name was Marian—never seemed to be at any pains to conceal the boredom that overcame her every time he put more than two words together.

It might have been that his being so slavishly attentive had been the attraction. Watching them together, however, I could never help thinking that, whatever the mysterious way in which he'd caught the fair Marian, all that

slavish fawning was now a desperate effort to hold on to
her.

I couldn't imagine that she was at the party, and I
hadn't seen her. It was not conceivable that, if she had
been there, he would have attached himself to that bevy
of Mrs. Thomases and been so long away from her side.

I was on the point of asking after her, but at that moment Allegra joined up and completed the group. Her arrival saved me from making a gaffe. It didn't fall to me to
introduce her to her predecessors. Adams took care of
that, and they all fell to persuading her of their theory. It
wasn't Tommy, it was someone else, someone playing a
practical joke, most probably Patience and Dodo.

Allegra was not easily persuaded. She was reluctant to
part with her certainty that she was being persecuted by
their common ex-husband. The suggestion that the practical joke might have been perpetrated by Patience and
Dodo, either or both, she rejected out of hand.

"If they had been playing this game," she said, "they
would have asked Marian, wouldn't they?"

Adams turned beet red and his lips trembled. With an
effort he pulled himself together and turned on Allegra.

"Since it appears that you are bitchy enough, my dear,"
he said, "I'm beginning to think you wrote those letters to
yourself."

The accusation could not have been more feeble. It left
out of account the six spurious invitations. Obviously, if
Allegra had not received a genuine one, she would have
been without a model for having the counterfeits done.

Allegra was quickly contrite. She dropped her hand on
Vernon's arm.

"I'm sorry," she said. "You're right. I shouldn't have said that."

I drifted away. My curiosity had been aroused, but I wasn't inclined to follow Allegra's route. I could take my questions elsewhere. I took them to Dodo, and that meant I fell into Patience Grimm's clutches. Before she could get started, however, I did slip my question in.

"What's with the Adamses?" I asked. "Didn't you ask her or didn't she come? I'd never have thought he'd come to a party without her."

"He surprised me too," Dodo said. "I didn't really expect he'd come. He hasn't been going anywhere since."

"Since what?"

"You haven't heard? Where have you been, Bag? Don't you keep up on anything? Everybody knows. She's left him. She's out in Reno establishing residence."

"People are saying he caught it from that partner of his," Patience volunteered.

"From Tommy? He caught what?"

"Wife losing. What else?"

"We couldn't ask her if we were asking him, and we couldn't not ask him," Dodo explained. "We've only known her the little while since their marriage, and we've known him ever so long. Anyhow, it doesn't matter because she's off in Reno."

"These people and the messy way they run their lives," Patience growled.

It was obvious that she had no moral objections to divorce; it irked her only because it created problems in the all-important realm of the guest lists.

"I'm furious with Ham," Dodo said.

"Who's Ham?" I asked.

"Don't be tiresome, Bag. You know him, everybody's ex."

"Oh, of course. Tommy."

He had always been Tommy Thomas to everyone who knew him. I suppose Dodo was the only person since his mother who never forgot that he was christened Hamilton Thomas.

"The additions to your guest list?" I asked.

"Oh, that. It was a fun idea. I only wish I had thought of it. Of course, they think I did, and it's so brilliant that I really wanted to take the credit, but Paysh keeps opening her big mouth."

"I'm going to get to the bottom of this," Patience growled.

"Nonsense," Dodo told her. "Getting to the bottom of things is the most useless thing anybody can do. So you get to the bottom. What then?"

"And the next time you give a party?" Patience asked.

"I'm looking forward to it. We shall have to do another one right away. Now there will always be that touch of unpredictability. It's delicious."

"Since you're so happy about the whole thing," I said, "why are you furious with Tommy?"

"He ran out on it. He lost his nerve. He took away at least half the fun."

"Not all of them remember what their envelopes were like," Patience said, "but a couple of them did notice. It was that same disgusting typing."

"Plus Allegra's letters," I said.

Patience could have been posing for an allegorical painting, serving as the model for both her names. She was the perfect picture of a relentless woman who was biding her time.

In the face of Dodo's determination to laugh the whole thing off, Patience served me up with the full details of her outrage. She was half ready to concede that the unbidden six hadn't actually crashed the party. They had had their cards after all, though she did insist that they should have known that the invitations were bogus. She wasn't prepared to say that they had known it and had come anyhow, but it was evident that she was thinking it.

"Now they're accusing me of sending them out. They're saying it was Dodo's idea and that I executed it for her. Can I be expected to hold still for that?"

"All of them? Allegra too?"

"Allegra too," Patience growled. "The only difference is that she thinks Thomas was in it as well, and the three of us were in cahoots."

"Maybe you'd better forget about getting to the bottom of her," I suggested. "She's carrying a gun. It's loaded and she boasts of being a sure shot."

"Don't I know it? She's been showing it to everyone. I've been telling Dodo. That's probably why Thomas didn't stay."

"Nonsense," Dodo told her. "Nonsense" has always been one of Dodo's favorite words. "Ham's a bastard, but he's never been a coward. He thought he was being funny, getting them all here and leaving me to cope with them. He stayed just long enough to make sure that all six of them had come, and when he saw there was going to be no fireworks, he got bored with it and pulled out. Just wait till I catch up with him."

"You'll spit at each other, Rolls to Rolls," I said.

"He drives a Jaguar," said Dodo, as though there was only that to stand in the way.

"If it was clear that he did it," Patience said, riding her own obsession, "it could be simple. Allegra was sure it was his typewriter and his typing, but Vernon Adams says that typewriter broke down completely and he got the fool a decent electric. So unless he typed the envelopes before the old machine broke down, I don't know."

"Vern is Ham's best friend," Dodo said. "Why wouldn't Vern lie for him?"

The rest of the time I stayed at Dodo's party I was involved with other people, and I was dismissing the whole deal as much ado about nothing. The six women had come together. They were started on what looked to be the beginning of a beautiful friendship. What all too evidently must have been intended as a cruel practical joke had not worked. Nobody had been hurt; and Dodo, who might have had reason to be incensed, was merely amused.

Patience, of course, was aroused. Nothing was going to stop her from probing and snooping, but even if she did succeed in getting to the bottom of the silly prank, there was not going to be anything much she could do about it beyond speaking her mind—and then it would only be if Dodo was too lazy to muzzle her.

Even Allegra's gun and her crazy letter had, I was thinking, been drained of all possibilities of ominous significance. The letters alone she might have thought to be a threat, but once she found out about the six invitations, she couldn't help but see them as only a part of some fool's nasty joke. She had every reason for taking offense, but it could hardly go on being a shooting matter.

I can't say I expected I would hear no more of it. I could well imagine that, in the event that Patience succeeded in uncovering something, Dodo would find the discovery so hilarious that she would have to fill me in on it, me and everyone else. But apart from that, I expected nothing, certainly nothing immediate.

When I pulled away from the party, I went to meet Inspector Schmidt for dinner. We went to my place afterward and I filled Schmitty in on what he had missed at Dodo's, and he made it clear that he felt he hadn't missed a thing. Schmitty takes a dim view of the very rich. I've heard him all too often on the subject.

"Money gives them too much power," he says, "and it doesn't give them any sense. They're adult delinquents, the lot of them. You don't hear about half the trouble they get themselves into because they're always buying themselves out of things and they're always getting stuff hushed up, but it's there."

It was only when I told him about Allegra and her gun that he showed anything more than the most languid interest. He scowled.

"That," he said, "is not funny. There's too good a chance she wasn't kidding."

"She's just a silly woman," I said. "Tommy was there for a while. She saw him, and in spite of her brandishing the pistol, she wasn't going after him. She was avoiding him. All she was doing was making a big noise."

Schmitty shook his head.

"You can never count on it," he said, "not if it's Texans and not if it's a domestic altercation. Do you know how high the husband-wife murder rate runs down there? You'd never believe it, and it isn't in the slums. It's in the his-and-her-limousine set, which is also the his-and-her-handgun set."

"I've heard," I said, "but Allegra and Tommy aren't married any more. She divorced him."

Inspector Schmidt allowed a hope that divorce might make a difference.

"Maybe she's not as Texan as she claims to be," he said. "Just the fact that she divorced him, that's encouraging. Down there they don't go to the courts to break up a marriage. They go to the six-guns."

Shortly before nine, long after we had dropped the Thomases and had turned to talk of other things, my telephone rang. I picked it up and I was considerably astonished and more than considerably irritated when I found that it was Patience Grimm calling. If grilling me was to be part of her way of getting to the bottom of things, I wasn't having any. I was ready to tell her off.

"Allegra," she said.

"What about Allegra?" I snapped.

"She's done it!"

"Done what?"

"She's shot him. He's dead."

"Tommy?"

"Of course, Tommy."

"Where are you?"

"At his place."

"Is she there?"

"No. After all, they were divorced."

"What are you doing there?"

"Calling you. Do you have to ask so many questions?"

"Have you called the police?"

"No. I called you."

"Why?"

My question about the police was all Schmitty had to hear. He moved off into my bedroom. I knew he would be picking up the extension out there.

"Why?" she snapped. "The way you're acting, I don't know why."

Schmitty had been in time to catch that.

"Hang up and call the police," I said. "That's the first thing you should have done, but, since you didn't, do it now—immediately."

"What do I tell them?"

"Tell them that a man's been shot and he's dead. He *is* dead?"

"He's dead. I found him that way."

"Do you want me to come over?"

"Me? No, not particularly, but Dodo will."

"She's with you?"

"No, but later. She'll want to know why I didn't call you. I suppose that's why I called you in the first place. I knew she'd say it's what I should have done."

III

I hung up and started toward the bedroom. Schmitty met me halfway. He had his shoes on. Before he said anything, I knew we'd be going over to Tommy's place. Long before I ever knew him, back at the beginning of the brilliant career that took him up through the departmental levels to the eminence of Chief of Homicide, Inspector Schmidt had been a rookie cop. That was back in the old beat-pounding days. Schmitty had pounded his beat, and his feet have never recovered. The inspector puts on his shoes only when he is ready to move.

"Your Texan," he growled.

I was quick to disclaim her.

"She's nothing of mine," I said.

"The dame who called you? Who is she?"

"Patience Grimm, Dodo's secretary and general factotum. You can call her Ms. Efficiency."

"She sounded like a dope. Do you think she's doing what you told her to do, making the call?"

"I don't know. I guess so. She's always been big on doing the correct thing."

"You offered to go and hold her hand. You know the place?"

"Tommy's house? I've been there."

"Okay, then," Schmitty said. "Let's go."

The house is a little one in the East Thirties, a block or two east of anything you could call Murray Hill. It once had been the Thomas carriage house, which is another name for a stable. If you look up accounts of old New York, you'll find descriptions and pictures of the Thomas mansions. Way back when, there had been five of them, all big and grand, ranged in a row along Madison Avenue. There had been five Thomas brothers in those days, all with large families.

By the time I had first known Tommy, however, all that had been long gone. The large clan had dwindled down to only Tommy himself. The houses had been demolished many years before, and a big office building stood where they had once been. Since this had been done before Tommy was born, the deal had been handled cannily: the ground along Madison hadn't been sold. The rent that had been coming to Tommy under one of those ninety-nine-year leases had, I always understood, provided a considerable part of his not inconsiderable income. I wondered a bit where the money would be going now. Since all six of his marriages had been childless, the Thomases were now extinct. Tommy had been the last twig on that tree.

I knew that his childhood, when he wasn't away at school, had been spent in hotels. His parents had always been on the move, sometimes jointly, more often separately, and he once told me that the only permanent thing he had known in his boyhood had been the old stable. By that time it had been converted into a garage for the family cars, and the two stories of dwelling space above it, earlier occupied by servants, had been standing empty. His great childhood friend had been a family chauffeur, and Tommy had spent much time playing in those empty rooms upstairs.

It was during his days at Yale that he had fixed up the two stories above the garage as bachelor quarters for himself. Ever since, in marriage or out, he had kept the place. Each time he had married there had been a new home, and each time he was divorced there had been a property settlement that gave it to the lady, and Tommy returned to his bachelor quarters. Whether the fact that he always had this familiar and comfortable place to go back to contributed to the fragility of his marriages I wouldn't know.

I am convinced, however, that the availability of such arrangements may well account for the high incidence of divorce among the affluent. For poor people it might require a major break for either one of them to undertake the crippling expense of moving out and setting up a separate establishment. Forced by economic necessity to remain together under the one roof, they find that proximity wears down the edges of their wrath and they make it up.

We were going there in the inspector's car. I didn't have the exact address at my fingertips, but I knew the street and I'd know the house when I saw it. It wasn't the only one of its kind in the city, but it was the only one on that East Thirties block.

There were some small loft buildings that housed furniture manufacturers' showrooms, and there were rows of old brownstones that had come down in the world except for their street-level space, which had been done over into arty little shops. Above those ground floors they were mostly slum flats except where they had been tackily modernized or where they were massage parlors.

Schmitty headed for the street I indicated. He carries the whole of Manhattan Island in his head. Hand him any address and he can immediately conjure up for himself the look, the smell, and the sound of the place, along with figures on the incidence of crime for the area, violent and otherwise.

"Alimony payments to six dames," Schmitty said. "I guess nobody's so loaded that he could swing that and have enough left over for a decent place to live."

"It's a great place," I told him. "You and I should only have it so good."

"Down there and east of Second?" the inspector said. "That good I don't need it."

I filled him in on the carriage-house deal, but he wasn't convinced. He had known people who had lived over garages who couldn't wait until they could move to a better place. I explained that it wasn't a public garage.

"It's just for his own car," I said, "and that's a Jaguar."

"In that neighborhood? Didn't he get mugged every Monday and Thursday?"

"You'll see the body," I said. "A mugger would think twice before trying anything on him. The guy was big and he was built."

"Somebody didn't think twice before shooting him."

"You were saying earlier that Texans don't think twice."

"You think she did it?"

"That's what Patience said. The gal was gunning for him. She was making no secret of it."

"Yeah," Schmitty muttered. "It can be, but it also can be that she talks and somebody else takes her talk for a screen and cashes in on it. Somebody else acts."

I tried to picture that.

"One of his other exes?" I said, just trying the thought for fit.

"Any reason to think so?"

"No. The way they looked to me, they were all rid of him and happy about it, no hard feelings."

"What about the dame who phoned you?"

"Patience Grimm? Why would she?"

"She's the one who wasn't taking it as a joke, wasn't she? Wasn't she the one who was plenty mad?"

"Killing mad? No, Schmitty, not nearly."

"Anyone else you can think of?"

"I can't even think it of Allegra," I said. "I'm sure she was just play-acting."

"I've seen them where the gun went off by accident," the inspector said.

"If she's the sure shot she claims to be, it isn't likely."

Schmitty gave me the pitying look. I know that look. It comes my way whenever I do or say something that inclines him to despair of my intelligence. I catch that look more than occasionally.

"If she's the sure shot she claims to be," he said, "and she carries a gun to a cocktail party, it can mean only one thing."

"And what's that?" I asked.

"She's so sure of her marksmanship that she's overconfident and careless. To get him at a cocktail party, she'd have to shoot into a crowd of people, wouldn't she? Nobody does that but a dope who knows nothing about guns or a dope who is crazily overconfident."

"You've had cops who've done it."

"Cops are people. They are people who have to keep a

gun on them all the time. It's regulations, but I've never been sure it's a great idea. If a man's going to panic or lose his head, it'd be better if he didn't have a gun on him. Anyhow, there's no comparison. Cops live with guns. That's not the same thing as picking one up for a special occasion like a cocktail party."

"Maybe she lives with her gun," I suggested. "Texans do."

"Uhhuh."

The inspector left it at that. We were rolling into Tommy's street and I turned to look for the house. But Schmitty needed no help from me. It was the only building of its kind on the block, three stories with the big garage doors at street level. Also, it was conspicuously better built and better maintained than anything else in sight. We rolled past the RUBADUBDUB and the dubs who were going in to be rubbed, and the inspector pulled up just short of a rival establishment with a vaguely Egyptian doorway. That one called itself CHEZ NEFERTITTY.

As we came away from the car, a youth, who looked as though his mother during pregnancy might have been frightened by a Norman Rockwell magazine cover, moved to meet us. He had the cowlick, the freckles, the snub nose, the blue eyes, and the aw-shucks, country-boy awkwardness. With one hand he shoved a CHEZ NEFERTITTY flier at the inspector. With the other he pressed one on me.

Schmitty shouldered past him and I followed in Schmitty's wake. The kid was left with his two fliers undelivered.

"What's the matter?" he called after us. "Can't read?"

The inspector ignored him. He had other things on his

mind. He was growling about the local precinct. The street was bare of any indication of a police presence.

"Someone's going to have to get over there and kick some ass," he said. "They catch a murder squeal. When do they respond? The day after tomorrow?"

We had come more than a mile. The precinct station house was only one block away.

Passing the broad garage door, the inspector addressed himself to the small one alongside it. He rang the bell and we waited. Nothing happened. Schmitty stepped back and looked up at the windows. Every one was ablaze with light—even a row of small panes set in the top of the garage door. He moved back in and leaned on the bell. The kid with the fliers had retreated to the CHEZ NEFERTITTY imitation of a tomb entrance. He called to us from there.

"Over here," he said, "you can walk right in. There's always a welcome."

We went over to talk to the kid.

"A lady," the inspector said. "Did you see her come out of here?"

"Her?" The kid's tone dripped scorn. "She's in there. Take my word for it, mister. We've got better. Ours are debutantes. They rub for a hobby. That's the ball game here."

Schmitty returned to the door and rang the bell. We were kept waiting long enough for an ancient arthritic to have been up and down those stairs several times over. Eventually we heard the lock turn and Patience opened the door.

I don't know what I had been expecting of her. She had never seemed the hysterical type, but I suppose I had been expecting at least some small measure of disarray, some little sign of distress.

She showed nothing. She seemed to be completely her usual crisp and efficient self. She was even carrying her customary air of disapproval and contempt.

"Must you be so impatient?" she said. "I heard the bell the first time. I was going to answer it."

"In your own good time," the inspector growled.

"In my own good time," she growled right back at him. "I was busy."

"Busy with what?" Schmitty asked.

I had shut the street door behind us and the three of us were standing crowded together in the tiny downstairs vestibule. Patience ignored the question. She spoke past him, addressing herself to me.

"Who is this lout?" she asked.

"This is Inspector Schmidt, Chief of Homicide, New York Police Department," I told her.

"I might have known," she said.

She wasn't moving. She blocked the stairs.

"Where's the body?" Schmitty asked.

"Upstairs in the living room."

"You've called the police? How long ago?"

"I called Mr. Bagby."

"I know that, but what about the police?"

"I was letting that wait until Mr. Bagby got here and he could make the call. He knows how to talk to those people."

"And you've been too busy messing around here?"

"I can't see that it makes any difference," she snapped. "You're police and you're here."

"Lady," Schmitty said, "I can't believe you're for real."

"Whatever that means," Patience said.

"It means," Schmitty told her, "that so far you've done everything wrong. I've always thought it would take at least two people to be that wrong."

"That," she said, "is only *your* opinion."

She was smug. She sounded as though she might have been waiting for a time when Inspector Schmidt would be compelled to eat his words, and she was showing every confidence that such a time was going to come.

"We'll have to go upstairs," Schmitty said.

"Obviously," Patience murmured as she started up the stairs before us.

She led the way to the big living room. Except for a small kitchen at the front, the whole of this lower of the two upstairs floors was occupied by the living room. Insulated by the kitchen from all sight and sound of the street, it gave the effect of being miles away from the scene down below.

I knew the room. It came to me as I entered it that this would be the seventh time I had been there. All the previous occasions had been parties known as Tommy's Independence Day parties. None of them had been given on the Fourth of July, though. They were in celebration of Tommy's, and not the nation's, independence. Each time a Thomas wife had been granted a divorce, Tommy had thrown one. They were always stag dos and they were always brawls. Each of them left the place pretty thoroughly wrecked.

By the next party, however, Tommy invariably would have everything put back exactly as it always had been.

It's always been my experience that if I wreck anything and I want to replace it with its exact duplicate, I'm told that the model has been discontinued and I have to settle for something else. Mysteriously, nobody ever seemed to have told Tommy Thomas that. It's the magic of money.

The place was expensively comfortable. It had everything a man could ever need and everything that few women would ever want.

That evening, of course, it had something that had never been there before, Tommy Thomas's dead body. The body was naked and it lay face down on a huge white bearskin rug. I remembered the rug. Nowhere else had I ever seen one quite that large. Naked and prone on that white bearskin, the body looked like an obscene and macabre travesty of one of those baby pictures.

The body was cold and it was showing the color of death, but, at first sight, I wondered how Patience could possibly have known that he had been shot. It took close inspection of the back to find the wound, and even then it was far from obvious. If it weren't for the small ooze of blood, it would have been all but invisible. After only the most brief examination of the body, the inspector asked the question.

"How did you know he had been shot?"

"I didn't, not until I came in here and found him this way."

"Okay. So how did you know it then?"

"I'm not a fool. It took no clairvoyance to see that the idiot was dead."

What was most obvious was that Patience Grimm took no stock in *de mortuis nil nisi bonum*. This was a gal who would carry rage, or even just pique, all the way to the grave and beyond.

"Dead, yes," Schmitty said, "but why shot to death?"

"She had a gun. And when I first came in, I could smell the burnt gunpowder. The fumes have dissipated but it has been quite a while since I first found him."

"Quite a while," Schmitty repeated after her. "I'd like you to be more specific. Just how long?"

She shrugged.

"I can't say exactly. The better part of an hour."

"It's been about fifteen minutes since you called Mr. Bagby. That leaves about three-quarters of an hour. What were you doing all that time?"

"Thinking most of the time, thinking and looking around. I was getting things pinned down for myself. I had to have that done before the police would be here and messing everything up."

If that got a rise out of Inspector Schmidt, he wasn't taking the time to let it show. He picked up the telephone and dialed the local precinct. It took him only a moment or two to set the standard procedures in motion. Hanging up, he returned to Patience Grimm.

"In your looking around, did you touch the body?"

"Of course I did. That was the first thing. I had to ascertain whether he was dead or alive. He might not have been past help, and if I could have detected even the faintest sign of life, a pulse, a heartbeat, a thread of breathing, I would have summoned a doctor."

"But you didn't need medical advice. Just on your amateur observations, you knew he was dead."

"I drove an ambulance in World War II. I'm something more than an amateur, Inspector."

"In your war service, did they give you any weapons training?"

"No, but I came to know the smell of gunpowder."

"How did you come to find the body?"

"I all but tripped over it when I came into the room. I could hardly have *not* found it."

"I can't believe that you don't know that isn't the question I asked," the inspector said.

"You asked how I came to find the body."

"All right, I'll play it your way. You came here. Was it by Mr. Thomas's invitation?"

"It was not."

"Had you told him you were coming? Was he expecting you?"

"I told him nothing. I don't know how long it's been since I last had occasion to speak to him. It's been months, I should say. What he might have been expecting I can't possibly guess, but it seems reasonable that he should have been expecting something as a result of his antics."

"Specify the antics."

She gave it to the inspector without the first word of qualification: Tommy Thomas had been sending threatening letters to the last of his six ex-wives. He had either stolen or reproduced six party invitations and had sent them to all six, although none of them had been on the guest list.

At that point the doorbell rang and Schmitty went down to open the door. Quite enough time had passed for precinct to be responding to his call, but I had expected that there would have been sirens to herald their arrival. I'd heard nothing and, until Schmitty came back upstairs with the precinct detectives, I was wondering whether Tommy mightn't have been having another visitor. I had forgotten how successfully the intervening kitchen insulated the big living room from all street noises.

While the inspector was out of the room, I had a few words with Patience.

"You're out of your mind," I told her. "You've opened yourself up to every kind of suspicion. There isn't a man, woman, or child who doesn't know that you call the police immediately and you touch nothing."

"Nonsense," she said. "You'll vouch for me."

"That'll be the day," I said.

"You'll vouch for me. You may growl and grumble, but you will."

"Give me one good reason why I should."

"Dodo," she said. "She won't have it any other way."

"And what makes you think I could do you any good? The mess you've put yourself into, nobody can do you any good."

"Your inspector will be grateful for my assistance."

Schmitty was up the stairs in time to catch that.

"I will," he said, "but when do I begin having your assistance?"

"When you start asking questions that mean something," Patience answered.

Inspector Schmidt, however, postponed the questions. First he took time out to read Patience Grimm her rights. Perhaps he should have done that at the beginning, but perhaps at the beginning he hadn't thought of her as a possible suspect. Riding down in the car, however, he had brought up the possibility. I had, of course, vouched for her then, but I found it difficult to believe that my judgment could have weighed that heavily with him.

I had to assume that he was doing it as a necessary

prelude to beginning on the questions that would mean something. There was also the fact that now the precinct detectives were on the scene, and he could hardly allow himself to set them a bad example.

She heard him out and I expected that he would do what I had not been able to do—impress her with the gravity of her situation. I expected that she would now say no more till after she had had advice of counsel, but she fooled me.

"Now, what do you want to know?" she said.

"He was already dead when you arrived here?"

"I've already told you that."

"Was he alone?"

"When I arrived, yes."

"What does that mean?"

"It means that before I arrived there had obviously been someone here. He wasn't shot by remote control."

"But when you got here that someone had gone?"

"Precisely."

"You have a door key?" he asked.

"Do you mean a key to this house, a key to the door downstairs?"

"A key to this house."

"No."

"Then if he was alone and he was up here dead, who let you in?"

"I let myself in."

"Without a key, Miss Grimm? What was it? A pick-lock? A loid job?"

"The door wasn't locked."

"You rang and had no answer. So you tried the door

and found it unlocked. Is that what you are telling me, Miss Grimm?"

"I'm telling you that I rang and had no answer. Then I noticed that the door was standing slightly ajar. The windows I could see from the street were all dark. So I went in."

"You had no hesitation about walking into a dark house with an unlocked door, a house in a high-crime neighborhood?"

Patience almost smiled.

"I didn't think of it as a high-crime neighborhood, Inspector. From what I saw out in the street, I should have called the neighborhood rather low."

"You came in and then what?"

"I made certain that the door locked behind me. I suppose that was out of habit. People are so careless. I'm always coming after them to check locks and to turn out lights and things like that."

"Why did you come in? What were you planning to do in here?"

"It seemed a stroke of luck," Patience said. "I hadn't hoped to have such a good chance for searching the house. I couldn't let such a golden opportunity pass."

IV

Inspector Schmidt disregarded this tacit invitation to leap ahead. He was taking her through it step by step and doggedly he was holding her to his pace. He had her in the house and starting up the stairs. On the way up she saw that the house wasn't completely dark, there was light at the head of the stairs. Not ever having been in the house before, she had been ignorant of its layout.

She paused on the stairs and called Tommy's name. When she had no answer, she resumed her climb.

"By the time I reached the head of the stairs and was about to come into this lighted room, I was smelling the burned powder. So I wasn't totally unprepared for finding him as I did."

"Okay. You thought it likely that he had been shot. What made you so confident that you wouldn't find someone with a gun up here and waiting for you?"

"I'd rung the bell. I'd called up the stairs. Nobody had answered."

"And it would have been etiquette for someone to answer you?"

"It never entered my mind that whoever fired the shot would still be here. The door left unlocked downstairs seemed certainly to be an indication of a hurried departure."

It seemed to me that she had been so delighted with the chance to search the place that she hadn't given a thought to any possible danger.

She came into the room and she found the body. She had touched the body but only to determine that the man was dead.

"There was no question of knowing who he was," she said. "I recognized him at first glance."

Schmitty went to the head of the stairs and looked at the body from there. There was a closet just beyond the stairs and he stood with his back to the closet door, surveying the room. When he leaned back against the closet door, it clicked shut. Seen from that angle, the body lay with its face buried in the rug and so turned that even the little of the face that was visible, a curve of cheek and a line of jaw, could be seen only from the other side of the room.

"He was someone you knew with his clothes off?" the inspector asked.

"I may assume that you intend the question to be offensive," Patience said, "but never mind. The answer happens to be yes. We have given many swimming parties and for a considerable time now it has been nude swimming—he initiated it, in fact. He was a vain and silly man who thought his body was a thing of consummate beauty. He was always inviting people to feel his muscles. For anyone who was interested, he most particularly recommended his pectorals and the muscles of his back, his abdomen, and his thighs."

No one could have asked for a more comprehensive answer. The inspector led her back to her step-by-step narrative.

Satisfied that her host was dead, she went through the whole house, turning on lights in all the rooms and searching the place systematically.

"What were you looking for?" Schmitty asked. "What did you have to find before we got here and messed it up?"

"The evidence I'd come for. When I came over here, I thought I was going to confront him with what I knew and force him to admit that he was the one who was playing these irritating games. Since when I got here he was past admitting anything, there was nothing I could do except look for the physical evidence."

"What sort of evidence?"

She explained that she had hoped for copies of the counterfeited invitations. Since she had frequent dealings with print shops, she was certain that none of them would engrave a plate to run off no more than six copies.

"Oh," she said. "I suppose you could pay for having the plate engraved and then have them run off as few copies as you like. It's always been my experience, though, that, no matter how many copies I order, they always seem to run off at least a few extras and send them along. It's never been an undercount, and it's never been the exact number ordered."

"Tell me, Miss Grimm," the inspector asked, "why was it so important—important enough to make you break the law—that you find them yourself? Why couldn't it have been left to the police?"

"Because the police wouldn't have recognized their significance."

"Even if you explained it to us?"

"Inspector," Patience Grimm answered, "if I want to

be certain that a thing will be properly done, I do it myself."

"With your little F.A.O. Schwartz do-it-yourself-every-kid-a-Hawkshaw detection kit?"

Patience turned to me in exasperation.

"Really, George," she said. "Can't you do something about your friend? The man is incurably frivolous."

I said nothing. Schmitty ignored the comment.

"I must require that you turn over to me anything and everything that you found," he told her. "It's unfortunate that I couldn't have seen it the way it was before you messed around with it, but now I'll have to make do with whatever you've made of it."

"It's upstairs," Patience said. "All of it, far more than I had ever hoped to find."

She led us up the second flight of stairs, and now I was in regions where I had never been before. There were two bedrooms up there and two baths and, as in the living room below, they were insulated from the street by an intervening room at the front. Here it was a game room. There was a billiard table, and over to one side a table with a backgammon board inlaid into its top.

One of the bedrooms was all neatly made up, and its bathroom had an equally neat and untouched look. Obviously these would be spare quarters for times when Tommy might have had a guest staying the night. These, it could be assumed, would have been male guests.

The other bedroom wasn't as neat. Various items of clothing lay strewn about. Patience called our attention to them.

"He came home and undressed," she said. "Those things were what he was wearing at our party."

Something that looked to be far more pertinent was standing there in plain sight. I moved over to look at it. It was all on the top of a bedside cabinet. The top had evidently been cleared to make room for it. There was a second similar cabinet at the other side of the bed, and its top was conspicuously crowded.

There was a pipe rack filled with pipes, a tobacco jar, a cigarette box, an ashtray, a clock, a three-decanter tantalus complete with whisky, gin, and vodka, and a small stack of books. I might have been more flattered at seeing one of mine in the stack if I hadn't suspected that it had come to him from Dodo. Since, by his own admission, he never read, I could guess that he had just never thought of any place to put gift books.

Both cabinets stood open, but that had been Patience's work. Having found what she wanted, she had grown greedy and looked further, but she had discovered only that one of the cabinets housed a small refrigerator, the bar type that is mostly for making ice cubes and with space only for chilling a few bottles of wine. The other was a cabinet which held bar glasses and an ice bucket and such.

When the inspector came to the cabinets and she told him that it was she who had opened the doors, he interrupted her.

"Downstairs," he said, "where you were standing when you first saw the body there was a closet behind you. That door was slightly open. Did you open that?"

"I left it as I found it."

"You searched all over but not in that closet?"

"That closet was empty except for the bare hangers. Obviously it was used as a guest closet. I looked in and then

I set the door back just as I had found it, slightly open."

"You didn't do that with these cabinet doors."

"No, I didn't. You were ringing the bell and you were so impatient, so I didn't stop to shut them. I went downstairs to let you in. I can shut them now if you like."

"Never mind. You've done enough pawing over things. Leave them alone now."

Schmitty turned to the pay dirt. It was on top of the bar-glass cabinet. It consisted of a portable typewriter, more ancient, dirtier, and more beat-up than anything you are ever likely to see this side of a junkyard. There was a piece of paper rolled into it and some typing on the paper. While Patience and the inspector were talking about the cabinet doors, I had been reading it.

> THE QUICK BROWN FOX JUMPS OVER THE LAZY DOG.
> the quick brown fox jumps over the lazy dog.
> 234567890-1=½;¢/,.
> "#$%_&'( )*!+¼:@?,.

Alongside the typewriter sat the other evidence Patience was saying she'd found. There was a stack of the engraved invitations to Dodo's party. Alongside it there was another stack of paper. For the moment that one baffled me. It was made up of THOMAS & ADAMS letterheads. The letterhead wasn't familiar, but it was the standard business form used by any outfit that wants its stationery to speak for its eminence and dignity.

They weren't the full sheets, however, but only the printed upper segment of the sheets. There was no space for writing. My first thought was that they might be samples of stationery that was to be made up, but I had never known a print shop that offered a customer samples in that form. They always let you see the full sheet to give you an idea of the look of it.

But it took no extended thinking before I recalled the letter Allegra had shown me. I had noticed the peculiar shape of the paper, something like eight-and-a-half by eight-and-a-half. It had seemed an odd size, but not if you thought of it as the standard eight-and-a-half by eleven with its top sliced away.

"Now, here," Patience volunteered, "is the evidence I was looking for, except that I never dreamed that I would find this much."

The inspector turned to me.

"Somebody told you that the old typewriter had been junked and replaced with a new electric," he said.

"That was Vernon Adams, his partner. He said this one was a hopeless wreck, beyond repair."

"It is," Patience said. "Look at the kind of copy it turns out."

She indicated the quick brown foxes.

"It's readable," the inspector said.

"It's a mess," Patience told him.

Schmitty came back to me.

"The way you told it," he said, "it was so bad that it wouldn't work at all. Did I get that wrong?"

"No," I said. "That was my impression. As I understood it, it had been years since it had last worked at all decently, but the kind of typing it did satisfied Tommy. I heard that he'd gotten rid of it only when it had reached the place where you couldn't work it at all."

"It doesn't work," Patience said. "The shift lock is broken. If you want to do a succession of caps, you have to hold the shift key down and type with only one hand. It also doesn't line-space. You have to turn the roller by hand."

Schmitty glared at her.

"You've been messing around with it."

"I tried it out to make certain that it was the machine that typed the envelopes. It is."

"Then these foxes are yours?"

She pointed to the sliced-off letterhead tops.

"I took one of those pieces of wastepaper," she said, "and tried the machine on the back of it."

"Where did you find all this stuff?" Schmitty asked.

"Just where it is," Patience said. "I moved nothing except for picking up the one piece of paper and rolling it into the machine."

"For a guy who liked his comfort," Schmitty said, "that's no comfortable place to type."

You can picture it for yourself. The cabinet top was at table height, but when you sat down in front of it you had no place to put your legs. You'd either have to poke at the keyboard awkwardly at arm's length, or you'd have to fold your legs in under you and type in the lotus position. Patience evidently was not impressed with the inspector's observation.

"If it matters," she said, "he typed so seldom, and if you look at his typing, you can see that he was never comfortable with it."

"It matters," Schmitty told her. "It may be important."

"Addressing the invitations mightn't have been much," I added, "but that letter Allegra had was a long one and she said they'd been coming like that one a day. For even a good, fast typist, doing a letter like that on that machine would have taken an hour or more. For Tommy it would have taken a lot longer. For Tommy that was a hell of a lot of industry."

Carefully the inspector lifted the typewriter off the cabinet and set it down on the floor. He did the same with the stack of invitations and the stack of sliced-off letterheads, baring the cabinet top. It was covered with a light film of dust, just about as much as the New York air deposits on any flat surface in the course of a single day. There were dust-free areas, areas that had been protected by objects that must have been sitting on the cabinet top through most of the day.

Neither the size nor the shape of these areas conformed to the size and shape of the typewriter or the two small stacks of paper. The inspector walked around the bed and studied the objects that crowded the top of the other cabinet.

He picked up the pipe rack and the tobacco jar. There was dust under them. Carrying them back around the bed, he set them neatly on the two dust-free areas to which they exactly conformed. There were two more dust-free areas, but Schmitty didn't trouble to fit them with their congruent objects. One would have taken the ashtray and the other the books.

"See what I mean, Miss Grimm?" he said.

She looked scornful.

"Ought I to be impressed?" she asked.

"I was hoping you might be enough impressed to recognize that it's no use lying to me."

"What would I be lying about?"

"That," Schmitty said, "would be something you know, and I have to find out."

"I am not in the habit of lying, Inspector, and I have no reason to lie."

"Maybe so, Miss Grimm, but you are not easy to believe. Perhaps I have to convince you of that."

Taking her story apart, he called it an impossibility, or at the least a gross improbability. He told her that she had been in the house a long time and she had been busy all of that time.

"You found so much you had to do here that even when we arrived, you were a long time answering the doorbell because you were still busy."

According to her story, she had been all that time looking for evidence, but, she said she had found it out in plain sight and all neatly assembled in one place for her. On the evidence of the dust, furthermore, it hadn't been there long and everything else had been cleared off the cabinet top so that it could be set out there on display.

"It has to be one of two things," the inspector said. "Either the time you claim you spent searching was given to doing something else here that you prefer not to tell me about, or else it did take a long search to find what you were looking for and you gathered it together and set it out on exhibition. Why you should not want me to know where you found your evidence I can't imagine."

Patience rose to new heights of scorn.

"It happens there was a third thing," she said. "I was going on the assumption that, if I was to find anything, it would only be by digging it out of some place where it had been carefully hidden away. Once I came on the body and realized that I had an opportunity to search, I set out to do the whole place exhaustively. I went through the lower floor systematically and I found nothing. I went down to the garage and I searched there. I hadn't quite finished in the garage when I came up here. I needed the car keys so I could check the trunk. I came up here for the car keys. I would, of course, have come after I finished with the garage, but once I was here, I saw what I was after. I didn't have to search any more. But that's where the time went. I was wasting it looking downstairs."

"Just when did you break off your search to call Bagby? Before you found what you wanted or after?"

"I called him as soon as I found the body."

"Oh, come on."

"There was no answer. I started searching and I didn't think about it again until I was up here searching the other bedroom. When I finished in there and I had still found nothing, I remembered that I had been trying to get George and I picked up the phone in there and dialed him again. That was the time I got him."

"So after you talked to him, you came in here and found that you didn't have to search. Everything you wanted was laid out for you in plain sight. Is that your story, Miss Grimm? Nothing there you'd like to change?"

"That, Inspector, is what I did and when I did it."

"Back at the beginning you said the windows in the front were all dark. You thought you were coming into a dark house till you started up the stairs and saw the light from the living room."

"You have a good memory, Inspector."

I might have said that these were the first words she addressed to the inspector that weren't scornful, if I hadn't had a strong hunch that the implication she intended was that he had nothing else.

"That is what you said?"

"That is the way it was."

"When we got here every window out front was lighted and there were lights on in every room in the house, front and back."

"As I've told you, I searched the whole house. I could hardly search in the dark."

"You also said a while back that you're in the habit of going after people to check locks and turn out lights. After other people, Miss Grimm? Not after yourself?"

That touched a nerve. The color came up hot in her cheeks. Patience Grimm was blushing.

"I was alone in the house with a dead body," she mumbled, making her words only barely audible. "I wanted lights."

She was confessing to a weakness. She hated doing it. She had to force the words out. I knew that she was never going to forgive the inspector for making her do it.

"Natural enough," Schmitty said, "far more natural than your choosing to stay here with the body, but you still have me confused on one point. You came up here because you needed the car keys so that you could check out the trunk," he said.

"We've been through all that."

Schmitty ignored her interruption. "Once you had found what you were looking for, you didn't have to find the car keys. You didn't need to go back down to the garage to look in the car trunk."

"Obviously."

"You came up here to find the car keys. Instead of coming into this room, the one place where you could expect to find them, you went looking in all the other rooms first. That room up front, for instance, his playpen. If I was looking for a man's car keys, I'd look in the pockets of his pants before I tried the pockets of his pool table."

"Oh, that. Once I was up here, it seemed silly to troop back down to the garage when it would be next to certain that I was going to have to come back up to search these rooms."

"Okay, now back to the matter of lights," Schmitty began.

"Oh, no, Inspector, not that again."

"Just a detail, Miss Grimm. You came into what you thought was a dark house, but you found that the lights were on in the living room downstairs. Was there any-place except the big room downstairs where you didn't have to put the lights on, any other room you found already lighted?"

"Yes, Inspector, here. This bedroom. That's why I came in here last. I had it so fixed in my mind that anything I could hope to find would be hidden away that I suppose I turned to the dark places first because they seemed more secret."

"Understandable enough," Schmitty said. "That brings us to when we arrived downstairs. You were a long time answering the bell because you were busy up here. What were you busy with then? You'd found what you wanted. You'd already finished in the other bedroom when you called Bagby. Am I right in thinking that immediately after you'd spoken to him you came in here?"

"Yes. That's what I did."

"You came in and right off you saw what you'd been

looking for. Then you tried out the machine. How long did that take you?"

"Seconds. I type rapidly."

"But when we got here you weren't through searching. I know that from the two cabinet doors you left open. You couldn't have been looking in there before you found the typewriter. The typewriter was right there in front of you. What did you find that you're not showing me?"

"Nothing."

"What were you looking for?"

"I honestly don't know. Possibly it was the gun."

"I must ask you to explain that."

"I was waiting for George to get here. As long as I'd been keeping busy, I had been all right; but, just waiting, I found it was suddenly getting to me that I was alone in the house with the dead body downstairs. So I just went on doing what I had been doing. I searched his closets and bureau drawers, not looking for anything, just keeping myself busy, filling in the time. I had just pulled the cabinet doors open when you rang the bell."

"And you hurried away from them without even shutting them, but still you kept us waiting. What were you busy with then, Miss Grimm?"

For the second time she blushed. I was ready to believe it was only the second time in her life. Again she resorted to mumbling. I had to strain to hear her.

"I wasn't busy," she confessed. "Suddenly I was frightened. I knew I'd called George and I could assume it would be him or possibly the police if he had called them, but my nerves had been coming to pieces. I thought, 'Suppose it isn't George or the police.' I was petrified."

Overcome with humiliation, she blurted it all out. Instead of going down to answer the bell, she had dropped everything at the first ring and had gone to the front windows, the windows of that room the inspector was calling the playpen.

"I tried to see who it was at the door," she explained. "I couldn't at first, but when I saw George, I was all right. I came down and let you in."

"You searched the whole house and you say you didn't find the gun?"

"That's right. I found no weapon of any kind, unless you want to consider kitchen knives, pool cues, or a tire wrench in the garage."

"You were looking for weapons?"

"I was looking for the typewriter. My search was exhaustive. If there had been weapons I would have found them."

"One more question," Schmitty said.

"Only one more, Inspector?"

"For now. When your nerves went to pieces, why did you stay on up here? Why didn't you go down and wait for us out in the street?"

"In that street down there, Inspector? Can you ask?"

"I can ask," Schmitty said. "Can you answer?"

"You had ample time to see the street while you were ringing the bell, Inspector."

"There are two policewomen downstairs," Schmitty told her. "They will have to search you."

"That, Inspector, you will have to take up with my lawyer. I would like to make my call."

"It's your right," Schmitty said. "The policewomen will wait with you until he gets here."

"I'm not submitting to being searched until she gets here, and then only if she says I must."

"Who is she?" Schmitty asked.

"My lawyer."

V

Leaving Patience, the body, and the scene of the crime to the precinct detectives and to his homicide specialists, who had by that time joined them, Inspector Schmidt, with me trailing after him, took his inquiries out to the street. The youth we'd encountered on our way in was still out there pushing his CHEZ NEFERTITTY fliers. As was to be expected, he was having a thin time of it. The patrolman stationed at Tommy's door, along with the police cars that now filled the street, constituted an inhibitory presence.

Schmitty lit a cigarette and strolled over to talk to the boy. Anyone who didn't know him might easily have thought that he was taking a break from his duties, but I knew better. When Inspector Schmidt takes a break from one of his investigations, he's not likely to do it with his shoes on.

"Sorry about all this," he said to the kid. "We're bad for business."

The kid laughed.

"At the moment, yes," he said, "but our regulars won't leave us. They'll be back another night, and think of all the future business we're picking up. We've already got a good crowd come to watch, and tomorrow it'll be bigger. Even the cops alone . . . that's a lot of business right there. I've seen cops here tonight who've never been around before. As soon as things quiet down, we'll be getting a lot of those and we won't have to give them any discounts like the precinct guys."

Schmitty grinned.

"Don't kid yourself, son," he said. "We'll get a line on you from the precinct guys. We'll know the going rate."

The kid put his full lung capacity into a mock sigh.

"You can't win them all," he said. "There's a law of economics that says there's no free lunch."

"A boy like you," Schmitty said. "What do you want with this grungy job?"

"It keeps me in gin for my soul, junk food for my belly, and jeans for my ass, not to speak of shelter and books and girls."

"There must be lots of jobs where you could do better," the inspector said.

"Name five."

"Hell," Schmitty said. "How would I know? You're intelligent, you've got education: it shows in the way you talk. You've also got gall. That shows in the way you act. With all of that, you could be a success at anything you wanted to take on. Guys who have far less on the ball are making it big."

"The bitch goddess success?" The kid laughed.

"What's wrong with it, son? You wouldn't be out here on your feet in all kinds of weather. You'd be inside, sitting down."

"If I'm inside, I want to be lying down, and for me it's not even discounts. I get mine on the house. The job? It's part-time and it isn't taxing. Also, it's educational. It gives me raw data to think about."

"You going to school?" Schmitty asked.

"Grad school. This is an earn-while-you-learn deal. Before I took this on, I had a part-timer selling cars, used cars. I could have stayed with it and gotten rich, but who wants it? I needed this to balance out my dissertation. It's a comparative analysis of the used-car and used-dame markets. It's going to be the first Ph.D. thesis to break into the best-seller lists."

"What are you studying?"

"I'll give you three guesses."

Schmitty shrugged. I did his guessing for him.

"Sociology."

"Give the man a cigar."

"That includes criminology," the inspector said.

"It can, but for me it doesn't. I gave that the pass except for a look at police statistics. Mind if I say they stink?"

"No skin off me," Schmitty said. "The numbers aren't my baby. I'm Homicide."

"Glad to know you, Homicide. It figures. I hear from the cop on the door that big, rich, and beautiful got himself knocked off."

"This evening. You been out here all the time?"

"All of it except for coffee breaks and piss calls."

"Any comings and goings over there, you'll see them?"

"The street's full of comings and goings. I don't take notice of all of them. I'm interested in prospects. Keeping tab on him or on his visitors wouldn't have done me any good, not for my work here and not for the dissertation."

"We went over there," the inspector reminded him. "You noticed us."

"Only when it looked as though you weren't going to

get in. I began thinking you might be prospects. If you were left with an evening on your hands, maybe you'd want to spend it somewhere."

"You noticed the woman."

"I'd never seen any woman go there before, and I'd never seen him bring a woman home. I had him pegged for a gay. So at long last a woman—that was something to think about. I came to the conclusion that from the look of her he could still be gay. After all, he lived right here and he never used any of us local tradesmen." He drifted off into talking to himself. "Tradesmen?" he murmured. "Tradeswomen? Tradespeople? Tradespersons?"

"Earlier, before she came, did you see another woman, coming or going?"

"Here in the street? Hundreds, I suppose. I take no notice of them. They're not prospects." He paused for a moment's thought. "I can't expect you to believe that now, can I?" he said. "Of course, there is the occasional one, specially delicious and exactly to my taste. I find myself making an exception."

"Very interesting," Schmitty said, "but not much good to me."

"You don't have to be *that* polite," the kid said. "Actually, it could hardly be more boring, another man's fantasies, another man's daydreams."

"Meanwhile what's your name?"

"You can call me Spike. What do I call you?"

"Inspector Schmidt. I want your full name."

"Okay, brace yourself. It's Euclid. Euclid Mallory. Mom was a mathematician and she wanted to call me Pythagoras, but the old man told her if she did, she'd have to have another so he could have the naming of it, and he was going to call it Pons Asinorum. I've never known whether it was the threat of the name or the threat of his knocking her up again that broke her down. They compromised on Euclid. If you are tempted to say anything like, 'I love my wife but, oh, Euclid,' skip it. I'm told that the penalty for assaulting an officer is stiff."

When we returned to the house the inspector was moaning.

"Not my night," he said. "A smart-ass dame and a smart-ass kid and I've got Six-gun Sister of San Antone still to come plus all those other wives."

"You won't find any of them like Patience," I told him.

"Like her?" he said. "I would hope not. There can't be another like her."

The boys had been working the house and had come up with nothing we hadn't already had from Patience.

"Looks like nobody stripped him down," the fingerprint lads said. "He undressed himself. Only prints we can bring up on any of the clothes he left strewn around the bedroom are all his own."

"Yeah," the inspector said. "We've been told. He was big on that, stripping down."

We went up to see Patience. The two policewomen had her upstairs in the spare bedroom. For the first time since I've known her she was having nothing to say.

One of the policewomen spoke for her.

"She made her phone call and, on advice of counsel, she's saying nothing. She said that much when she came away from the phone and not a word since, not even about the weather. We're waiting for her attorney."

"She been fingerprinted?" Schmitty asked.

"She refused fingerprinting, Inspector."

"Without talking?"

The policewoman turned to look at Patience and turned back to the inspector.

"Like that, Inspector," she said.

Patience needed no words. She was sitting on her hands and shaking her head.

The inspector walked away, but he didn't get far. We were still on the stairs down to the living room when the attorney arrived. She introduced herself as Mrs. Brent, and she looked as though she could be in competition for the title of Grandmother of the Year. She had a lot of silver hair disciplined into a massive bun at the back of her head. Her face was round and full and built for smiling. Her glance impressed me as sympathetic, and she had a fine shelf of bosom ready for crying on.

"Where is my client, Inspector?" she asked.

"Upstairs, Mrs. Brent. I'll take you right up to her."

"I understand that she was advised of her rights somewhat belatedly."

"At the very first moment when it developed that there was even the remotest possibility of her being a suspect. She showed no interest in her rights. She submitted to questioning without any protest. It was only when she heard that she would have to be searched that she asked to make the call she could have made anytime. Did she complain of being denied her rights?"

The smile her face was built for broke out. She tried to suppress it, but she couldn't quite manage it.

"Her only complaint, Inspector, was that the questioning was interminably long and boring."

"Could you tell your client, Mrs. Brent, that we are not in the amusement business?"

She nodded sympathetically. "The easiest clients, Inspector," she said, "are the confirmed criminals. They know how to behave when they are in the hands of the police. It's the innocents who give an attorney a headache."

"If you don't mind my saying so," Schmitty told her, "your client would be anyone's headache. If she isn't the stupidest intelligent woman I've ever come up against, she's working at being the smartest. You could do both her and me a favor if you impressed on her that it's a bad idea to get smart with the police."

"Please take me to her, Inspector," Mrs. Brent said.

I waited on the stairs while the inspector took her up. He was quickly down again, bringing the two policewomen with him. Mrs. Brent had been left alone with her client.

The two policewomen had opinions.

"She's a man hater," one of them said.

"We know the type," the other added.

"I know her," I said. "She's an everybody hater—men, women, children, dogs, cats, and horses."

"Cold as ice."

"Anything that one did would have to be premeditated."

"No sudden impulse for that one."

"No heat of passion."

"I pity anyone that crossed her."

"Sex-crazed if you ask me."

"No loyalty to your sex?" I asked.

To me they'd been sounding too callow and too glib.

"We are police officers," they said loftily and in unison.

"But never detectives," Schmitty muttered as we came away from them.

"You take no stock in their estimate of their fellow-woman?" I asked.

"Too soon and too little evidence for all that conclusion jumping," he said. "And they're doing it on nothing but the look of her face and the way she sits."

"So what do you make of it?" I asked.

"We've got one bit of evidence that might hold the answer to the whole thing," Schmitty said. "I'd say that it does if I could only be certain of just how phony it is. It's phony, there's no question about that, but so far we have no way of knowing just how phony."

"And what's that?"

"The stuff she says she came here to find, the typewriter and those invitations she says are faked copies. Why were they set out there on that bedside thing? Who put them there and when? They hadn't been there long."

"I saw that," I said. "When you picked up the typewriter and the paper, there was dust under them and no less dust than on any other part of the exposed surface."

"That's it," the inspector said. "Even if they had been set down on an already dusty surface, there would have been a noticeable difference in degree of dustiness."

"Then, what are the possible meanings?" I asked.

"Those cut-off pieces of the letter paper," he said. "They must mean something, but I can't imagine what—not yet."

I broke in on him and told him about the peculiar shape of the paper used for the letter Allegra had been displaying at Dodo's party.

He gave me the big grin. He whacked me on the back and told me I was great stuff.

"That's important," he said. "At the moment it isn't helpful, but it's important. It at once strengthens the thing and weakens it."

"So hooray for Bagby," I said. "But what does it all mean?"

"The typewriter, the invitations, and the sliced-off letterheads were put there on exhibition," the inspector said. "The easiest answer is Patience Grimm. She's lying. She found them hidden away somewhere and she brought them out to show them to us."

"Why would she lie about it?"

"Won't admit that she tampered with evidence."

"But she did admit to trying out the typewriter and she admitted to having been into everything, searching."

Taking her behavior apart and putting it back together again, the inspector demonstrated just how she could have reached a place where she felt she had to feed him a combination of truth and lies. He reminded me of how emphatic she had been in denying that she had in any way tampered with the corpse. She had touched it only to the extent that she had to if she was to make certain that he was dead. She had admitted freely that she had searched the house.

"She would have preferred to pretend that she hadn't," Schmitty said. "I can imagine how she kept changing her mind. She had found the typewriter and the paper and, in her excitement, she made the mistake of taking them out to examine them. She could have put them back and left them for us to discover."

"Why didn't she?" I asked.

"Because everything she did here was idiotic. After she did it, though, she got to thinking, and then she realized that she'd have a lot of explaining to do. After all, she had been seen coming into the house."

"Yes," I said. "If she tried to lie about how long she had been here, there was little chance she could make it stand up."

"Exactly. She was going to need some explanation of what she'd been doing all that time, and she couldn't think of anything better than the simple truth. She'd been searching the place from top to bottom, and we were going to find her fingerprints all over everything. She hadn't thought of that till it was too late."

"She could still have put everything back," I objected. "She could even have told us where to look. She hadn't disturbed anything, she hadn't tampered with evidence—she had only searched. She'd left everything for the police exactly as she had found it."

"With those quick brown foxes in the typewriter and some of her fingerprints on the keys?"

I wasn't out of objections.

"Granted," I said, "that she couldn't go over the whole place, but she could have given the typewriter a good wipe and she could have pulled her foxes out of the machine and flushed the paper down the john. You'd have no way of knowing how many pieces of that letterhead there had been."

"If she had thought of it," the inspector conceded. "On the other hand, she might have decided it was safer to leave them and say she'd found them there. Then all the tampering she'd have to admit to was trying out the typewriter."

"That was such a natural thing for her to have done that she thought we'd expect her to have done it. Apart from being technical about it, does it matter all that much?"

"If all she's guilty of is delay in reporting a murder and this minor bit of mucking around with the evidence," Schmitty said, "it doesn't matter much. What makes it matter is, first of all, the possibility that she's telling the truth and that somebody else set that stuff up to be found. If it's that way, it will mean a lot. Then, there's the other thing. It can't be ignored."

"Like what?"

"Suppose she's the one who shot him and she set all this up to point to that Texan ex of his. That's not impossible. If a woman goes around making threats and brandishing a gun, she's sucking around for a frame."

"You're thinking that Euclid saw no other woman come in here," I said.

"I'm thinking that Euclid said he saw no other woman come in here," the inspector amended. "I wish I could believe the kid. But there's too good a chance that he has himself set up in the blackmail business."

"He saw someone and he's holding out because he expects more profit in blackmail?"

"After all, Baggy, what did he give us? He saw Patience Grimm come into the house. Since we were about to find her in here, he was giving us nothing we weren't going to have without him."

He had spoken as though he'd been seeing multiple possibilities. I was about to ask him about the alternatives, but I had to check myself. Mrs. Brent came down and brought her client with her.

If I was ever to see a chastened Patience Grimm, I was seeing her then. From the look of her, she might have been crying on her counsel's ample bosom. I found it difficult to believe, but if she hadn't been weeping, it would need to have been a sudden attack of hay fever.

"This little girl behaved most foolishly," Mrs. Brent began.

I wondered if ever before anyone had called Patience Grimm a little girl. The universal facts of growth and development made it necessary to recognize that she must have been one once, but I could never visualize her as an infant or even as a child. The best I could do was a miniaturized Patience Grimm, formidable, wry, and efficient.

The inspector refrained from comment, and the attorney went on with it.

"She tells me that she gave you a full and detailed account of her every action," she said.

"Was that foolish?" Schmitty asked. "She must have told you that she confessed to nothing substantive."

"She made a full and frank confession of everything she did. You could ask no more of her."

"There is more I have to ask of her," Schmitty said. "Just a couple of small things, but they are necessary."

"Please specify, Inspector."

"First that she consent to be fingerprinted."

"Is that really necessary? After all, on her admission, you know that you are going to find her fingerprints all over the place."

"Just what makes it necessary, if only so that her prints can be eliminated."

"I see," Mrs. Brent said. "I'd like to withdraw with my client and discuss it."

"Suppose you postpone that," Schmitty suggested, "till you've heard the rest. Then you can discuss the whole package."

"Yes, Inspector. What else?"

"She will have to be searched."

The lawyer nodded.

"My client told me you were demanding that. We consider it unwarranted."

"The man was shot. The weapon has not been found. Your client was here before us and she admits to having searched the whole house."

"Are you prepared to charge her with the killing?"

"I am prepared to charge her with withholding information of a killing. She had ample time and she never called the police."

"She called Mr. Bagby."

"Not the same thing. Calling George Bagby is not what the law requires. I am also prepared to charge her with tampering with evidence. You are aware, counselor, that I can take her in and book her and that then the fingerprinting and the search will be automatic. I won't need her consent."

"Am I to understand, Inspector, that you are using the threat of arrest to exert pressure on my client?"

"You are to understand, Mrs. Brent, that short of dereliction of duty, I am making every possible effort to discomfit and inconvenience your client as little as possible."

"Then, if she submits voluntarily to the fingerprinting and the search, you will consent to my taking her out of here?"

"Unless something is discovered in the search to make it a new ball game."

"Such as, Inspector?"

"Such as the murder weapon, or any other incriminating object."

The two women went back upstairs and, after a very brief huddle, they returned. Patience was saying nothing. She was leaving it to her attorney to speak for her. I could well imagine that this enforced silence might have been for her the most traumatic aspect of the whole experience. She was enduring it with ostentatious stoicism.

"My client," Mrs. Brent said, "makes no objection to the fingerprinting. She will also submit to being searched, but, since I have been closeted alone with her, I demand that I be searched as well and that the fact of it should be established in the record."

"I thank both of you," Schmitty said.

The fingerprinting was quickly done, and attorney and client retired with the policewomen. The search took a little longer, but nothing was found. Patience took off with Mrs. Brent, and I thought that would be the last of that.

It wasn't, though—not quite. As soon as they had departed, the inspector had his men repeat their search of the room where Patience had been alone with the attorney.

"Once she knew she was going to be searched," Schmitty said, "she'd know she had no hope of getting away with anything. If she had something she didn't want us to find on her, she'd get rid of it."

"Suppose she flushed it down the john?" I asked.

"Even the smallest handgun won't flush," Schmitty answered. "You know that."

"I was thinking of paper," I said. "Letters or some such."

"Connecting her with the dead man?"

"I don't know," I said. "I hadn't thought that far."

Schmitty gave me a quizzical look.

"Think as far as you can, Baggy," he said.

"Nowhere to go with it," I said. "It was a silly idea."

In terms of Tommy Thomas and Patience Grimm it was more than silly. I hadn't the faintest idea of what manner of man Patience might go for, if any. On his track record, however, there could be no doubt about which way Tommy's inclinations ran. Nothing could have been more absurd than the thought that they could ever have run to Patience Grimm.

But whether or not her purpose in coming to the house that evening had been the one she claimed, I very much doubted that she had been acting on her own behalf. There were, of course, things that she would do for herself—like sleeping, eating, and breathing—but, apart from such, I could think of nothing she had ever done that had not been done for Dodo.

These things were not always on Dodo's orders or at Dodo's request. I had known her to do things over Dodo's most emphatically expressed objections. If Patience Grimm thought a thing was good for Dodo, she did it whether Dodo liked it or not. When I mentioned letters, therefore, I hadn't been thinking of Patience and Tommy —I was thinking of Dodo and Tommy.

Why, then, did I back away from telling Inspector Schmidt what had been passing through my mind? It was a conflict of loyalties and I didn't know how to resolve it. Dodo was an old friend. In her own absurd fashion she had over the years done me many a kindness, and I reproached myself for even having had the passing thought. I should have hated myself if I had spoken it.

VI

The search yielded nothing. The inspector and I pulled out and left the technical specialists to finish working the place. Schmitty waited until we were in the car before he spoke. Even then, it was only after he had eased out of his shoes.

"The six-gun babe out of Texas," he said, "any idea where she lives?"

"Peculiarly enough, I do know her address."

"What's peculiar about it? You buddy with the whole gang of them, don't you?"

"Buddy with them? No," I said. "I knew Tommy. We were friendly enough, but we never were buddies. You should know that, because you never met him. Anyone I'm really close to, if he lives here in town or even if he comes through at all frequently, you've come to know him. It's inevitable the way you and I are in touch practically all the time."

"With him it was Thomas or the wives? Was that it?"

"It really wasn't anything," I began.

"Since you know where she lives, tell me and let's get going. While we're riding, you can tell me just how it wasn't anything."

I gave him the address. I had it complete, street and number.

"You know it better than you knew his place," Schmitty commented.

"Peculiarly enough," I repeated.

"You been seeing her since they split?"

"Only this afternoon at the party, but that was it. They had me up there a couple of times while they were still living together."

"I know the house number only because I had a couple of refreshers on it this afternoon," I said.

"She wanted you to come over? She been making a play for you?"

"If she had any such ideas, she kept them well-concealed. No. There were the two envelopes, the one with the crazy letter and the one with the invitation. They were addressed to her at the apartment where she'd lived with Tommy."

"If Grimm has leveled with me," Schmitty said, "then it has to be the killer who put all that stuff out on exhibition."

"To point suspicion at Allegra?" I asked.

"Unless this works out the simplest way," Schmitty said. "She might have gone over there to have it out with him about the threatening letters. She found the typewriter and stuff, or he brought it all out and showed it to her, taunting her with it. Either way, she got mad enough to shoot him."

"What about his stripping down?" I asked. "What would that have been for?"

"Grimm says he did it to show himself off. But he might also just like walking around bare-assed. He was home alone. She paid him a surprise visit, and he saw no reason for jumping into pants. On the other hand, he could have been teasing her with what she gave up."

"And she shot him in the back? That bothers me, Schmitty."

"Yes," the inspector said. "In the back and not up in the bedroom but downstairs. It bothers me too, but what bothers you about it?"

"I don't think it's in character for her. There's something sneaky about it. If she shot him, I think she would have wanted to see his face when she squeezed the trigger. She'd want him to know he was getting it."

"You could be right about that and it still wouldn't rule her out."

"Why not?"

"She pulls the gun on him. They're face to face. He thinks she's bluffing and he calls her bluff. He turns his back and he starts walking away from her. That gets her even madder and she squeezes off the shot. It makes better sense that way than figuring she'd go running around in front of him to get her shot off."

"If you see it that way," I asked, "then what is there to bug you about it?"

"It isn't that it makes it impossible or even unlikely for her to have done it," Schmitty explained. "It opens up another big possibility that I cannot ignore. Shot in the back always suggests a sneak attack, and there's that closet at the head of the stairs."

"That's what I meant."

"I know, but you can't call it proof. You get the picture of the killer getting Thomas in the back, with him never even knowing that he wasn't alone in the house. Put that thought together with all that stuff on display, and you have to think about a killer who's taken advantage of the way she'd been carrying on and is framing her for the killing."

"And since the gun isn't hers, leaving it wouldn't do the killer any good," I added.

"If it was someone else, perhaps," Schmitty said. "Of course, if it is this Allegra dame, she didn't leave it because it is her gun."

"Maybe she couldn't have done anything about the typewriter, but she could have gotten rid of the rest of it," I objected. "Why would she leave all that to point the finger at herself?"

"Isn't that what she said she was going to do? She said she was going to bring out all those threats and plead self-defense. The stuff out on display pins it down so that there should be no question about the threats having come from him. It's flaky, but just on what you've told me about her, I know the lady is a flake."

We pulled up at the house. It's a big apartment on Sutton Place. Nobody could ever say Tommy Thomas didn't do his wives well.

The doorman made a big deal of looking at his watch as he asked if we were expected. When we said we weren't, he looked at it again.

I looked at mine. To my surprise it was only just past twelve. It had been a long evening but it had started early. Inspector Schmidt doesn't go for any dinner-at-eight custom. He likes it early except when he is in the heat of an investigation. Then he'll grab something at any hour, if at all.

The inspector identified himself. That lifted the doorman out of his preoccupation with his watch. He moved to the lobby switchboard. After a moment or two he was back.

"Mrs. Thomas wants to talk to Mr. Bagby," he said.

I looked to the inspector.

"Go ahead," he said. "You can tell her I won't bite."

The doorman handed me a phone.

She didn't ask me why we had come. I had a feeling that she had been expecting us.

"George," she said, "come right up and bring your friend. There's just one thing."

"What, Allegra?"

"You've caught me in bed and that means naked. I've been sleeping for hours, so I'm wide awake—you didn't wake me or anything like that. I'll put something on, of course."

I told Schmitty.

"Sleeping for hours," he muttered. "What would the early-to-bed bit be for? She's already wealthy. From what you've told me about her, I'd guess she's healthy. Does she think one night will wise her up?"

I said nothing. I was thinking of the way Raskolnikov slept after he'd murdered the two women, but the thought seemed irrelevant. I couldn't picture Allegra as a Dostoevski character, and it seemed to me that in the great Russian's time Texans had hardly been invented. The inspector had something. On what I knew of Allegra Thomas, early to bed and early to rise was not her style.

She was at the elevator door to greet us. She had put on a nightgown and something over it, but the nightgown and the something enveloped her in nothing more than a diaphanous film. Her hair and her make-up were both impeccable, and her head had certainly not just come up off a pillow.

"You'll have to take your shoes off," she said by way of greeting. "Everybody has to take shoes off up here. It's the white rugs."

My first thought was that she might have heard somewhere about Inspector Schmidt's feet and she was thinking she had found a way to butter him up. The rugs, however, couldn't have been more dazzlingly white. They looked as though shoe leather had never touched them. She was barefoot herself, and her lacquered toenails in the deep-piled carpeting looked like a row of rubies in a snowdrift.

"Back down home," she went on, "it's because of the way spurs gouge the floors. Here it's the white rugs. I hope you don't mind."

"I don't mind," the inspector said, as he shucked his shoes.

I could see that he was working at tamping down his delight.

"Bourbon and branch," she said. "Or if you go for something else, just name it."

"Thanks, no," Schmitty told her. "Nothing for me."

"Oh, come. I don't believe that. You look like a man who enjoys his booze. Scotch? Cognac?"

"Not on duty, ma'am," Schmitty said.

She took a moment to think about that. The pause gave me my first opportunity for wedging in an introduction.

"Inspector Schmidt," she said. "Yes, I know. Howard said. Howard's the doorman. He's a pompous pain in the tail, but he does speak plainly. Of course, you've come about those letters. I might have known George would tell you."

"You should have reported them yourself," Schmitty told her.

She gave him a dazzling smile.

"I know I should have, but I never do as I should. Nothing could be more boring. Now, where shall we go to talk, Inspector, outside or in? It's a beautiful night. We can sit out on the terrace with all that moonlight and sootfall, or in here with plenty of light so we can study each other's faces and try to read each other's thoughts."

"In here, if you please," the inspector said.

In here was a couple of acres of living room. She had done it over since I'd last seen it, and the white rug was only a part of it. It was all white. Even the flowers—white roses, white carnations, and white freesia—were arranged in squat masses in milk-glass containers with only the blossoms showing, not a leaf or even a bit of stem to intrude the smallest spot of green.

She settled herself on a sofa and indicated chairs for us. She had it set up for a tight little huddle with all that empty white space around us.

"I suppose you'll want to see the letters," she said.

"First I would like to see your gun," the inspector told her.

"No good your confiscating it, Inspector. There are always more where that one came from. I have to have a gun. I've always had one. I'd feel undressed without."

"You don't have it on you now," Schmitty said.

"I'm not dressed. Don't tell me you haven't noticed."

"You're going to have to take this seriously, Mrs. Thomas."

She pouted. It was a mistake. She couldn't make it look genuine. It was a travesty of a pout done by someone who had never had a pout of her own and who had no talent for mimicry.

"Now you're going to lecture me and tell me that I mustn't shoot him. You'd do better to tell him to stop provoking me."

"The gun, please, Mrs. Thomas."

"I'll get it for you," she said as she rose from the sofa. "It's a sweet little gun. George has seen it. He can tell you."

Schmitty waited till she was out of the room before he spoke.

"Is she always like this or is she putting on an act?" he asked.

"She's not always like this," I told him. "She has a great variety of acts and she's always putting on one or another. This afternoon it was THE GIRL OF THE GOLDEN WEST. Tonight it's something she probably thinks is Noel Coward."

"She's never just herself?"

"If you ask me, she's been putting on acts for so long that she hasn't any self left to be."

Schmitty sighed.

"A nonstop phony," he said. "This room. Alone in a white world. When will she go into her NANOOK OF THE NORTH act? Does she rub noses?"

"It wasn't all white like this when last I saw it," I said. "That was before the divorce."

"It figures," Schmitty said. "She's had it done over. Maybe she thinks her divorce gave her back her virginity."

"Like Jim Thurber's woman who always wanted to live

in the past, so she went to the Virgin Islands for her divorce."

The Thurber reference got me a small smile.

"Now that you've met her," I asked, "what do you think?"

"Supercool, or she didn't do it."

"Can anyone be that cool?"

"With her long experience in putting on acts, why not?"

We lapsed into silence and the silence lengthened. Allegra was staying away a long time. The inspector checked his watch. He paced the room. After he had crossed and recrossed its vast reaches several times, he checked his watch again.

"A woman who must always have her gun on her," he said, "should know where she put it when she undressed. She's one helluva long time finding it."

"Unless it's taking her this long to lose it," I suggested.

"Or to clean it," Schmitty added.

He started out of the room and I followed after him.

"Any idea of where in this white wilderness the bedroom would be?" he asked.

I showed him the way. I had some recollection of the general layout of the penthouse. I had never been in any bedroom part, but I could steer him away from the dining room and the other areas they had used for entertaining.

We came on her bedroom. It was as unrelievedly blue as the rest of the place was white. It was a cold blue that could have been an ice cavern. The door stood open and she was sitting on the bed. She wasn't doing anything. She was just sitting there.

"Forget what you went for, Mrs. Thomas?" Schmitty asked.

"Call me Allegra," she said.

She said it mechanically, as though her mind wasn't on it.

"The gun, Mrs. Thomas."

"Yes, Inspector. That's just it—the gun. I've been sitting here trying to think."

"Nothing to think about. You are going to have to hand it over."

With my talent for irrelevance, I found that the moment for wondering whether Allegra belonged to the National Rifle Association. She made none of their characteristic noises.

"That's the problem, Inspector. I can't think where I could have put it."

"Where do you usually keep it?"

"In my purse. George can tell you I had it in my purse this afternoon."

"Then, you don't keep it on you here in the house?"

"Ordinarily? No, I don't."

"What does 'ordinarily' mean? When *do* you?"

"Living alone, there's no point. If certain people were coming to visit, of course, I'd take care to wear something with a pocket."

"Who are these certain people?"

"I suppose I should have said a certain person. I was thinking of my former husband."

"Mr. Thomas?"

"He was my one and only."

"When do you last remember seeing the gun?"

"This afternoon at Dodo's party. That's Dodo Baines.

George knows her. He was there, but, of course, you know that. George saw the gun and that's why you're here."

"It's part of the reason."

"Yes, I know, the gun and the letters."

"They're part of it too."

"And the idiotic prank with the invitations. I didn't think you'd be interested in that bit of ill-natured silliness."

"I'm going to have to be interested in everything about you, Mrs. Thomas," Schmitty said. "It would be a good idea if you listened carefully to what I now have to say and paid close attention."

Then he read her her rights.

I think she listened carefully. I think she paid close attention, but that, too, could have been an act. She looked as though she were all but hanging on his lips. I had to wonder if she could actually be that much absorbed in the formal words.

She waited soberly enough until he had finished. Then she gave him the dazzling smile.

"Inspector," she said. "You've got to be kidding."

Schmitty came right back at her.

"Mrs. Thomas," he said. "You've got to be serious."

She rose from the bed.

"A bedroom, Inspector, is no place for you and me to be serious in, certainly not with George here. If we're going to be serious, I'll be happier back in the living room."

She led the way.

Settled back on the sofa, she again indicated our chairs.

I sat, but the inspector remained on his feet, standing over her.

"Beginning with the time you left the party this afternoon," Inspector Schmidt said, "you will tell me in complete detail where you went and what you did."

She giggled.

"And that can be used against me, Inspector?"

"Come on, Mrs. Thomas."

"If you call me Allegra, I'll call you Schmitty."

"Mrs. Thomas," Schmitty told her. "I can put you under arrest. I can take you in and dump you in a detention pen while I go about the other things I have to do and until you are ready to answer questions properly. If you want it that way, you can have it that way. It'll be a lot easier for me. I've been trying to treat you with consideration. You've been trying to make it impossible."

"Sorry, Inspector, but it just seems too silly."

"Regardless of how it seems."

"We all left Dodo's together and we spent the evening organizing the club. Then I came straight home and went straight to bed. That must have been about an hour before you came—just time enough for undressing and putting things away neatly. I'm compulsively neat, Inspector. Then I brushed my teeth and popped into bed only to pop right out again because Howard called from the lobby to say you were here. Ask Howard what time I came in. He'll know exactly. Howard's a great one for knowing the time."

I thought the inspector would pick her up on the contradiction. She had been sleeping for hours and now she hadn't slept at all. He let it pass. It seemed evident to me that he was going to let her hang herself.

"'We all left Dodo's together,'" Schmitty said. "Who are 'we'?"

"We've only just organized. We haven't a name for ourselves yet."

"Who left Dodo's with you? Who organized this club?"

"Oh, all of us, all six. He's going to have to do it again and twice. We can't just go on forever talking about him. Two more will give us two tables for bridge."

"Mr. Thomas's former wives?"

"Yes, Tommy's six exes. We do need a name. Tommy's six exes, we don't like that at all."

"What about the Thomists?" I suggested.

Allegra liked it. It got me a scowl from the inspector.

"You left together and you were together all the time?"

"Well, togetherish."

"What does 'togetherish' mean?"

"You can't get six into one taxi, so we had to split up three and three to go down to Louella's house. It was Louella, Charlotte, and Constance in one taxi, and Agnes, Claire, and me in the other. We're doing it this way till we get to know each other better, nobody thrown together too much with her immediate successor, so that no hard feelings crop up."

"You went to the first Mrs. Thomas's house? Louella? She was the first, wasn't she?"

"She was, and why she wasn't a warning to the rest of us is one of those mysteries we're going to try to fathom."

"When you got to the house, it was the six of you together?"

"Yes, Inspector. The six of us were together all evening until we broke up and went our several ways."

"You all left together?"

"The five of us. Louella didn't have to leave. She was home already."

It seemed to me that she was just gagging it up with these overmeticulously precise replies, but I couldn't be sure. I had sat in on other questioning sessions where someone brimful of withheld guilty knowledge worked at setting up a false appearance of candor by being just this hair-splittingly honest about trivialities.

"What time did the five of you pull out?"

She went into a deep study.

"What would it have been?" she mumbled. "Eleven-ish? Something like that. A cab from West Ninth Street up here, that would be a half hour or a little less. I had to walk down to the Fifth Avenue corner to find a cab, and I waited some. I'd say easily a half hour. On your way out, Inspector, ask Howard what time I came in and subtract about thirty minutes from that. You'll have the time when I left Louella's."

"No dinner?"

Obviously Inspector Schmidt had no interest in whether they had eaten or not. He was just testing.

He got more response than he could have wanted. They had had dinner, and very good too. That was the advantage of the Village—all those wonderful little shops, and you could call them any hour of the day or night and they delivered—the hot things hot and the cold things beautifully chilled and everything ready to eat. She was seriously considering selling the penthouse and buying a place down in the Village.

She ran on about the manifest advantages of life in Greenwich Village, and I wondered how long Inspector Schmidt was going to hold still for it. Any way you looked at it, it was a peculiar performance. She had just been read her rights, and, from her reaction, it was obvious that she had been aware of the significance of the reading.

Even on the assumption that she had no knowledge of the shooting, she could still not have been ignorant of the fact that she was under suspicion and that the suspicion, one way or another, was connected with her missing gun.

For her to be showing no curiosity about what the inspector had in mind and to go on with this silly babbling seemed totally unnatural. This performance could either have come out of so comfortable a conviction of innocence that she didn't have the slightest worry about what the inspector might be thinking, or it had to be an act she was putting on to cover her guilt. If it was the latter, it seemed to me she was overdoing it. She might have been more convincing if she had shown some normal curiosity.

She had alibied herself admirably for the full span of time during which the shooting might have been done, and I was ready to call it an unassailable alibi. It depended on five women she had met for the first time that afternoon. Although they were women who had much in common, they could hardly have been regarded as old and trusted friends. What was to say that concealed under one or the other of the five fashionable coiffures there might not lurk all manner of concealed animosities? If that alibi was not genuine, then certainly Allegra Thomas was depending on five slender reeds. The very fact that it depended on so many as five witnesses was, of course, a strength if the alibi was genuine. If the alibi was false, however, it could be a fatal flaw. They were all going to have to be in agreement on every last detail of the story. Any slip from any one of them was likely to blow the thing wide open.

Thinking about it in those terms—and I had more than enough time to think while she was babbling about the goodies Louella had commanded from the local shops—I was forced to the conclusion that she was telling the truth. No woman could be fool enough to involve herself in so dangerous a lie.

Eventually she ran down. Falling silent, she looked to the inspector with a now-what-would-you-like-to-know expression.

"Now, this gun of yours," he said.

"I'm beginning to think I must have lost it, Inspector."

"Where?" Schmitty asked. "How?"

"I have this bag," she explained. "I was carrying it today. It's marvelously big, but it doesn't organize. Do you know what I mean?"

"Things tend to fall out of it and get lost?" Schmitty asked.

"Oh, no, not that. Things get lost right inside it. Whenever I want something out of it, somehow it's always at the bottom."

"You're not telling me the gun is at the bottom of the bag and you haven't gotten down to it?"

"That's how stupid you think I am, Inspector?"

"I'm trying to understand," Schmitty said.

"And I'm no help. I know it. I haven't George's gift for finding the words that make everything clear."

"Do your best, Mrs. Thomas."

"Allegra, please."

"All right, Al," the inspector said. "Do your best."

"You see every time I wanted anything out of my bag I'd find the gun in the way, the gun and all manner of other things. I kept taking it out so I could have it out of the way and get what I wanted."

"And?"

What she was trying to say was evident enough, but the inspector wanted it from her in her own words.

"And one of those times I must have taken it out and forgotten to put it back. I left it lying around at Dodo's or at Louella's. I suppose we can't call and ask if it's turned up in either place, not at this time of night, but first thing in the morning, unless . . ."

She stopped short and pressed her hand over her mouth. Schmitty waited. She brought her hand down and she finished what she had been about to say.

"Unless," she said, "I left it in the cab. I was fishing around for my money when I paid the cab driver. I don't remember doing any such thing but the way it was all day, I may very well have taken the gun out and put it on the cab seat beside me to have it out of the way while I dug down for the money. I bet that's what I did. I just left it in the cab." She brightened. "He was a nice cabby," she said. "He'll find it and bring it back. He'll know where he took me."

"I doubt that you lost it that late in the evening," Schmitty said. "If you lost it then, it was only because you wanted to lose it."

"That sounds Freudian, and the Freudian thing never did fit me. I fulfill my desires; I don't suppress them."

Discussions of Freud are not Inspector Schmidt's thing.

"You kept bringing it out in front of people. All manner of people saw it and knew where you carried it," he said.

"I wasn't ashamed of it, Inspector. It was a pretty little gun. I hope it comes back. I was fond of it. I suppose you think I was going around showing it off. Actually I wasn't."

"What were you doing, then?"

"Only being sensible and taking proper precautions. It was loaded, Inspector. I couldn't just keep pushing it around inside the bag, taking the chance of it going off by accident. I am an old hand with guns, Inspector. I know how to handle them and I'm most careful with them. I was just doing the proper thing, lifting it carefully out of the bag and setting it safely aside while I fished around in there for the stuff I wanted."

"It's going to be necessary to have this apartment searched," the inspector said. "Am I going to need a search warrant?"

"That's in case I didn't just leave it somewhere but took it out and have now forgotten where I put it," she said. "I wish you would, Inspector. Otherwise I'll have to do it, and I can think of nothing more boring. Of course, if I hear that it's turned up at Dodo's or Louella's or if the cab driver brings it around, I'll let you know. Do I reach you through George, or where can I call you?"

"I'll give you a number where I can be reached. Meanwhile I have to use your phone."

"Do, Inspector. By all means, do."

VII

Schmitty hit the phone and set it up for a search team to come to the penthouse. I expected that while he was occupied on the phone, she would have a try at pumping me, but not Allegra. She just made polite conversation. She was most grateful to me. I was a darling. So thoughtful of me to have brought the dear inspector around. She was falling madly in love with him. He was such a sweet and helpful man. He was a duck. He was a teddy bear.

"How's your Greek, Allegra?" I asked.

"My Greek? I never had a Greek."

"The language," I explained. "The Greeks called the Furies the Eumenides, and that means the well-disposed ones, and they called them that in the hope that they would be well-disposed."

"The inspector, George? You're being absurd. He is sweet and helpful. He's cuddly. I adore the man. Introducing him to me is the nicest thing you've ever done."

Schmitty came off the phone.

"I have a search team coming over," he said. "They'll be here in a few minutes."

"Oh, goody," she said.

She was overdoing it.

"You seem to have no curiosity about why I'm so interested in your gun," the inspector said.

"Curiosity? What's to be curious about. I know why. How could you not be?"

"You know why?"

"I've been carrying it around without a permit, and George told me this afternoon that it's against the law and you're an officer of the law and, now that it's lost or mislaid or whatever, there's no knowing who might pick it up and most likely a person who knows nothing about guns and won't know how to be careful with it and the most dreadful things might happen as a result. Of course, it worries you. Why wouldn't it, Inspector?"

"It may not have been your gun, but it's most likely that it was. Your former husband was shot this evening, Mrs. Thomas."

She gasped.

"Tommy? You must be joking. It's not possible."

"When loaded guns are around, a shooting is always possible."

"But Tommy tonight," she argued, "when every last person who could have had any reason for killing him couldn't possibly?"

"You mean yourself and the five who came before you?"

"Obviously. The six of us. Who else? To know Tommy was to love him. To marry him was to learn to hate him. We talked about that this evening. Charlotte has this cotton hat and it has a label in it that says 'guaranteed to fade.' She told us about it because she said it reminded her of Tommy and of marriage, and we all agreed that there ought to be a label like that on all marriage licenses issued to Tommy Thomas."

"Not even one tear for old times' sake?" Schmitty said.

"I'm a big girl, Inspector, and I'm from Texas. In Texas big girls don't cry. How is he?"

"He's dead."

She caught her lip between her teeth. When she released it, the lipstick had smeared.

"How awful," she moaned.

"You were threatening to do it yourself," Schmitty reminded her.

"Oh, that," she said. "I never meant a word of it. As a matter of fact, that's why I made so much show of the gun. I wanted the word to get to him that I was out gunning for him. I hoped that would scare him off that nonsense I thought he was annoying me with."

The search team arrived and the inspector put them to work. There was no suggestion that Allegra's person should be searched. After all, under that filmy stuff she had put on to receive us no gun could possibly have been concealed.

Although the search for the gun was exhaustive, it came up empty. It was an emptiness the inspector considered significant.

"You had threatening letters," he said. "The boys didn't find any."

"Oh, those. I never kept them."

"You had one this afternoon. You showed it around. You kept *that* one."

"Only through the afternoon. The girls convinced me that they couldn't possibly have been coming from him. So then they didn't matter."

"Threats always matter," Schmitty said.

"These threats cooked up to look as though they came from him?" she said. "Combine them with the invitations and the whole thing falls into proportion. It was some idiot practical joker, and the best way to handle those clowns is to ignore them."

"It looks like it was the worst way to handle this practical joker," the inspector said. "He should have been stopped before he got too practical, or do you think it's all for the best?"

"If there was ever a man who deserved killing, it was Tommy Thomas," she answered. "But that's neither here nor there. I'm sorry it happened. I suppose when it comes to the actual thing, you realize that nobody deserves killing. Talking about it is one thing and doing it is another. Doing it is wrong."

It was a different Allegra who spoke those words. It could have been that for a moment she'd allowed the real woman to surface. For once I had the feeling that this was not another of her acts.

We pulled out of there. Downstairs in the lobby the inspector stopped for a word with the doorman.

"Mrs. Thomas suggested that we ask you what time she came in tonight," he said. "She couldn't place it exactly, but she said you were good about things like that. You'd know the precise time."

"Mrs. Thomas? She came in at eleven-thirty."

"That's about the way she remembered it. Now, how about when she went out. Can you tell me that?"

"No, sir," the man said. "That I can't. I didn't see her go out. It must have been before I came on this afternoon."

"What time did you come on?"

"Five o'clock."

It worked out. It had been before five when I'd seen her at Dodo's. The times fitted her account of her movements. To that extent they were verification of her alibi, but, of course, they said nothing of where she might have been from the time she left Dodo's until eleven-thirty, and it was in that time that Tommy Thomas had been killed.

"You work a long shift," Schmitty said.

"My relief called in sick. I'm working two shifts."

"And during the time you've been on you saw her only the once, when she came in at eleven-thirty? She didn't come in anytime during the late afternoon or evening and then go out again?"

"I told you she didn't." The man's tone had taken on an edge.

"Yes," Schmitty said, and now there was an edge on his tone as well. "That's what you told me, and I'm thinking that's what she told you to tell me—me or anyone who asked."

"I'm telling you what I know. You can take it or leave it, but don't go calling me a liar."

"I'm not calling anyone a liar," the inspector said. "Not yet, I'm not. For now I'm just thinking."

The doorman shrugged.

"Nobody can keep you from thinking," he said.

"You know Mr. Thomas?" Schmitty asked.

"He used to live here when they were still married. It was when they began splitting up he moved out."

"Like him?"

"He was all right."

"You said 'was.'"

The inspector pounced on the word.

I expected the man would say he'd heard about the killing on the radio news or had been told about it by someone who'd heard it. By this time the news might well have been out. I didn't know whether it was or it wasn't, but the man didn't come up with that answer.

For a moment he searched for words. His dignity failed him. He looked like a man who'd been caught out and was beginning to squirm. It was, however, only a moment. He made a rapid recovery.

"He was all right," he repeated. "Since he moved out, he hasn't been back around here at all. When I knew him, he was all right."

Inspector Schmidt kept the exit line for himself.

"I'm still thinking," he said, "and it would be a good idea if you did some thinking too, like thinking about any times you might have seen Mrs. Thomas tonight. I may be asking you again."

We left the building, but to go only as far as the inspector's car. Settled into it and out of his shoes, the inspector lit a cigarette.

"What was all that for?" I asked. "All he told you was that she was out all through the time when Thomas could have been killed. He didn't alibi her."

"He gave me times that fitted her alibi."

"Yes, but if the alibi is a phony, she could have been anywhere this evening. She needn't have come back here."

"Right enough, Baggy, but if she did come back here, that would be the end of her alibi."

"What makes you think she did?"

"She makes me think it. She told contradictory stories

about having been asleep. She's having trouble remembering what to say. She made too much of a point of my asking this guy, Howard, just what time she came in; she was too anxious to have the time established and to have it corroborated. I can see no reason for her to want that so much unless she's faking it, and she has Howard primed to back her up. She's a generous tipper, wouldn't you say?"

"I'd say, and I can tell you another thing about her. She treats everyone with the same kind of matey breeziness. I guess that's the Texan in her. It works wonders with all the little people—servants, tradesmen, cabbies, delivery boys. It takes her only a moment and she has them at her feet."

"Yeah. Where do the other wives live? West Ninth, and she walked to Fifth for a cab. That means between Fifth and Sixth, so it's probably not an apartment but a house. There's no apartment house in the block, at least none that would be in their bracket."

I thought back. There had been too many in between, but I remembered. It was an unforgettable house, one of those beautiful old ones, small but perfect.

"Yes," I said. "It's a tiny house. He bought it for his first bride. It was very much the love nest, just big enough for two."

"And the others?"

"All over town—Central Park South, Fifth Avenue somewhere in the Seventies, Park Avenue in the Sixties, and Gracie Square. It was always a new neighborhood for a new wife."

"But none of them in the slums. The slum place he kept for himself."

"Not even anything as close as the good part of Murray Hill," I said. "Maybe even the first time he was already thinking he might need an escape hatch."

"Do you have the addresses, or am I going to have to look them up?"

I glanced at his dashboard clock before I answered.

"You're not going to do the rounds now and wake them all up?"

"People stay up to watch the 'Late Late Show.'"

"Not *these* people. At least, I don't think so."

"You could be wrong, but it'll wait for morning anyhow."

"We calling it a night?" I asked.

"Right away. There's just the one thing I want to pin down with you."

"What's that?"

"These places where they live. What sort of places are they?"

"You saw Allegra's. He did all his wives that well. There are differences of taste, of course, but they're all top fashion and top luxury."

"Not what I need to know. Allegra's is a penthouse apartment, and the first one was a small townhouse in a quiet street where there's no street life. I'm not likely to find anyone down there who was watching and who kept track of comings and goings."

"West Ninth in the evening? You never see a soul in the street."

"Right. Now, Central Park South—that's got to be an apartment. No townhouses along there, none for years now."

I nodded.

"I remember a terrace with a magnificent view of the park," I said.

"That leaves three. What are they? Houses or apartments?"

"As I remember them," I told him, "Fifth and Gracie Square were terrace apartments, and Park was a penthouse, but don't hold me to it. I may be mixing them up a little. Gracie Square might be the penthouse."

"It doesn't matter. Except for the first one, they're all apartments. That's what I need to know."

"That much I'm certain of. They are all apartments."

"All with doormen around the clock?"

"Co-ops in their price bracket? What else?"

"In theory," Schmitty said, "it could be inconvenient for a criminal, since there's always someone there to let you know if he's lying about his comings and goings. In practice I've found it not all that good. You know the big boys in the Mob with their snazzy Central Park West pads? You start questioning elevator boys and doormen about them and you come up with a big fat nothing. Their tenants keep them too well tipped and too well terrorized. You never can get anyone to talk."

"I hardly think the Thomas girls have their doormen and elevator boys terrorized," I said.

"But I'll bet they're great tippers. Nobody's going to tell us anything. We're going to have to wait around for the slip of the tongue."

"Like Howard just now?"

"Yeah. Like that."

I raised one small doubt.

"These places are the ones they had while they were married to Tommy," I said.

"You said he always moved back to his slum and left the little woman in possession."

"He did and with ownership as part of the divorce settlement, but that doesn't say they've all stayed put to live among their memories. They could have sold the apartments and set themselves up elsewhere. I wouldn't know about it if they had."

The inspector switched on the ignition and pulled away from the curb. He drove a few blocks and on Second Avenue he found an all-night bar with a phone booth and a not-too-mutilated telephone book. In that area, of course, it was a gay bar. Barmen and patrons stopped everything to look us over.

"They think we're a couple," I muttered.

"Better than coming in alone to look at the phone book," Schmitty said. "Do that and they'd think you were queer for telephones, and who wants to look that perverted?"

Checking the addresses took some time. Since they were all Thomases, we didn't have to flip all over the book. That, however, was the only part of it that was easy. None of them had their given names listed. Few women living alone in New York do. Thomas is not an uncommon name. Only on my memory of apartment locations was I able to pick Claire, Charlotte, and Constance out of a great run of C. Thomases, and Agnes out of a multitude of A. Thomases. I located all of them, and I was able to tell the inspector that, however ill-suited they might have been for marriage with Tommy Thomas, they had, every one of them, been well-suited to the shelter he had provided. None had sold. They'd all stayed put.

The inspector looked disproportionately happy.

"Good work, Baggy," he said. "I suppose in here I should kiss you for it."

"Let me just imagine it," I said.

We bellied up to the bar. Since he was knocking off for the night, the inspector was ready.

"I'm buying," he said. "It's the least I can do, since I'm not going to kiss you."

"Okay," I said. "In addition to Howard, who is so good at telling the time, you now have four sets of doormen to work on; but, if it's only that, you're liking it too much."

"It's a lot more than that. It's the pattern of the thing. It's one place out of six, and the only one of the six where they could have come and gone without witnesses. Add to that, they left the party together and with a choice of six places they could have gone to, they went to the one that was farthest off. That alibi isn't just phony. It's silly."

He waited till morning before he worked at it.

We started with Louella, hitting her early. Although she had had far more time for it, she had been less enterprising than Allegra. She had left the little house exactly as it had been years before when she had been married to Tommy. So far as I could see, she had changed nothing. At Allegra's the general atmosphere had been radically changed, but if there had been changes here, they had been kept unobtrusive. The general look was the same.

She was awake and working on the morning papers when we arrived. It was a big story and she had been absorbing it with both her eyes and her ears. She had her television on and it was pouring out the news. She brought us into the house and switched the television off.

"I've taken my phone off the hook," she said. "Reporters ringing till I thought I'd go mad. That's why you couldn't reach me and had to come unannounced. I'm sorry."

"That's all right," the inspector said.

He saw no need for telling her he had made no attempt to call her for an appointment or that appearing at her door unannounced was the way the game was played.

"You've come about Tommy, of course," she said. "It's a funny thing. I've always thought that one day this would happen, but I suppose in my heart I never really believed it would because, now that it has happened, it's been as much a shock to me as if I'd never had the thought."

"He had enemies?" the inspector asked.

"Tommy? God, no. Everybody liked him."

"Everybody?"

"He was the most likable man, Inspector. He was engaging the way a puppy is engaging."

"A puppy who is also a wife beater?"

Her first reaction to that question was to throw a reproachful look at me. She promptly, however, switched it to a smile and a shrug.

"Naturally you would know about that," she said. "George would have to tell you."

It was obvious that she would have preferred that it not come up; but, since it had to be discussed, she was prepared to handle it candidly and without resentment.

"That was puppyish, too," she said. "If you have ever owned a young dog, Inspector, you'll know what I mean. They'll nip at you. I have known them at times even to bite painfully."

"I know," Schmitty said. "It's like with kids. You work

at training them out of it and you wait for them to grow
up a little."

"Exactly, Inspector. I suppose that, in turn, that's what
each of us did." She caught herself up and amended that.
"All of us, I guess, except Allegra. She was his last. She
didn't wait. I'm inclined to think that makes her brighter
than the rest of us. It should have been obvious to all of
us that he was a big boy. There was no point in waiting:
it was too late for him to grow up."

"So you stopped liking him and you divorced him,"
Schmitty said.

She shrugged.

"Yes. When I said that everybody liked him, I suppose
that wasn't entirely true. There are the six of us and we
would be the exceptions."

She went on to expand on that to the extent of offering
him the comparison between Tommy Thomas and the hat
with the "guaranteed to fade" label.

"So he did have six enemies," Schmitty said.

"Not enemies, Inspector, just six women who had
learned to like him less. Oh, yes, there was a time just before we parted when I did hate him. It wasn't a killing
hate. It was more like an abhorrence, not wanting to be
around him, wanting him out of my life. Looking back on
it now, though, I can say that even in the moment of parting this feeling began to fade out. That was Tommy. He
was good at marrying and he was good at being divorced.
It was only marriage itself that he wasn't good at."

Schmitty permitted her to go on about it, and she explained. When the moment of exit came, Tommy behaved
so graciously and so gracefully that it became difficult to
go on hating him, and he continued in such fashion all

through the more often bitter business of property settlement and legal technicalities.

"We were talking about it only last night," she said.
"All six of us. I suppose George has told you that after all
this time we got together just yesterday. The others
thought he had done it so well with them because he'd
had previous experience, but it wasn't that. It was just the
way Tommy was. I was the first—he'd had no previous experience then."

"Yours was the first," Schmitty said. "You've had time
to forgive and forget. The last Mrs. Thomas . . ."

"I've forgotten nothing, Inspector. A woman doesn't.
You bring up Allegra. Since George was there, you obviously know about her gun and the wild threats she was
making at Dodo Baines's party. It seemed to me that she
was pounding on George about it more than on anyone
else. You must understand how that was, Inspector."

"I'd like to understand, Mrs. Thomas," Schmitty said.

It was an invitation to explain. She jumped at it. As she
saw it, Allegra had been no different from her predecessors. She had also been affected by his gracious handling of all the divorce business and had harbored no
hard feelings against him.

"But then she began having those letters," she said.
"Naturally, they made a difference. They made her very
angry. I can understand how she felt, but once she was
convinced that Tommy couldn't have been writing
them . . ."

The inspector interrupted.

"Was she convinced?" he asked.

"Oh, she was. I'm sure she was."

"There's evidence to say she might have become unconvinced," Schmitty said.

"I know. It's all here in the papers, the typewriter and the invitations and the printed tops cut off the letter paper. But none of that means anything, Inspector. It couldn't have been Allegra. All the accounts give the time when the police were informed that Tommy had been shot. Allegra was still here and she had been here all evening. So that's that, Inspector."

"Tell me about the evening," Schmitty said.

She told him, and in every respect her story matched the one we'd had from Allegra. From time to time the inspector interrupted to pin down a detail, but he was unable to bring out any discrepancies. The way they had divided up in the two cabs, what they had done about dinner, even what she had ordered in for them to eat—every detail was a duplicate of Allegra's story.

On a detail like who rode with whom in the two taxis, she was letter-perfect. They had split themselves up into noncontiguous trios, but such agreement in the two stories left the inspector unimpressed.

"That's like the stuff they teach in memory courses," he told me later. "They call them mnemonic devices. If you have stuff you want to remember, you try to arrange it in some pattern that will help you remember. What are the easy patterns to remember? The first three together and the last three together? That's easy but it looks contrived, and we might be wondering why they contrived it that way. Something random? That's too risky. One or the other of them might get confused and foul it up."

"So they're stuck with something that will sound contrived and they're smart enough to underline the contrivance. They offer us a good reason for why they rode that way."

"You're getting the idea."

While we were still with Louella, there was one item in the story that struck me. I hadn't picked it up when we'd had it from Allegra but when I heard it for the second time, it hit me. It wasn't anything that the inspector could have picked up, but it had me so bemused that I had trouble keeping my mind on the rest of what she was telling Schmitty. Since, however, he was satisfied that the two stories matched, I guess I didn't miss anything.

After they had been through all that, he took her back to what she'd said at the beginning.

"You always thought that one day this would happen," the inspector said, "but you were also so positive that he had no enemies. I don't understand that."

"That house, Inspector. In that neighborhood. It was a constant invitation to any criminal. The way Tommy looked, the car he drove, the way the house looked and everything around it so poor and slummy, it was just asking for it."

"You're thinking a thief?"

"What else? He surprised a thief and the man shot him."

"He came downstairs naked and he surprised a thief," the inspector said. "So he just turned his back on the man to go upstairs and get some clothes on? He was shot in the back."

"I know. That's what the papers say. The naked doesn't mean anything. Tommy spent most of his time with his clothes off. Even with people around, it never worried him. Another man, hearing someone downstairs, would have jumped into trousers before running down to investigate, but not Tommy. He just ran down the way he was, and the thief, lurking somewhere, didn't wait for Tommy to turn and see him. He just shot him in the back. He would. Tommy was so big and powerfully built, no robber would wait and take his chances on tangling with Tommy."

"There's no sign of forced entry."

"Don't they have keys or ways of opening locks? Don't the people who know about locks say that there isn't anything that's really burglar-proof?"

"Any lock can be opened," Schmitty said. "He had a good lock, and a good lock will show some signs of tampering."

"A skeleton key?"

"There's no indication that anything was taken."

"Money?" she asked. "The papers say nothing about money."

"There was no money, but there was a checkbook and all kinds of credit cards. Living the way he did, would he have any cash around?"

"Would he?" she said. "Unless he's changed—and I'll never believe that—there was money around. He never had less than five hundred dollars on him."

"Even when he was naked? Where would he be carrying it?"

"It would have been in the house, stuffed in his trouser pocket, lying around in his billfold. If it isn't, then I'm right. It was robbery."

As soon as we were out of the house, I filled the inspector in on what had occurred to me.

"The dinner she got in for the six of them," I said. "I

didn't think of it last night when Allegra was going on and on about all the things Louella could order in, but it's funny. Item for item they are the things that were served at Dodo's party. Not the caviar and not the champagne—I suppose that would have been overdoing it, but otherwise they're saying she ordered in all the things they'd just been eating at the party. Can we believe that?"

"We can't," Schmitty said. "It's another mnemonic device."

VIII

The program called for visiting the other four Mrs. Thomases, but before heading for the next lady on his list, the inspector, as was his custom, used his car phone to check in on whether anything had turned up for him. Something had turned up. The inspector had another killing.

The victim was a young man, a student named Euclid Mallory. He was dead of gunshot wounds, but this one wasn't the clean and efficient job that had been done on Tommy Thomas. Euclid had four slugs in him, all fired from the front. One was in the left shoulder, one in the left arm, two in the chest. The killer had wasted three shots before zeroing in on Euclid's heart.

"Messy," I said when the inspector passed the news on to me. "That doesn't look like any work done by sure-shot Allegra."

"You mean it doesn't look like the same marksman?" Schmitty asked. "I think you're wrong. More likely it's just the difference between front and back."

"What difference?" I asked. "A man will be as broad a target either way."

The inspector enlightened me. The way he was reading it, Tommy Thomas had been a stationary target.

"He either had no notion of what was coming at him," Schmitty said, "or he'd seen the gun and he was so sure it was just going to be waved around and not fired that he turned his back on it and just stood there offering an easy shot. Euclid was face-to-face with the gun when he got it. He was dodging and twisting. He'd have no delusion that it wasn't going to be fired. He knew it was in the hands of a killer. The odds are he was moving in and trying to make a grab at the gun. Under those circumstances it could easily have taken four shots to finish him off."

"Yes," I conceded. "That makes sense, and there's another thing. With Tommy it could just have been a lucky shot, and nobody is going to be lucky every time out."

"Of course," Schmitty said, "it puts Patience Grimm in the clear."

"How do you figure that?"

"What reason could she have for killing Euclid?"

"If we assume the killings are related?"

"It's the reasonable assumption. I never for a minute thought he was giving me everything he had seen last night. He stank of blackmail. So he tried it on the killer and he got his.

"But not from Patience?"

"From anyone *but* her. She was the one person he couldn't blackmail, and he knew it. There was nothing he could tell us about her that we didn't already know."

"I get what you mean. It would have to be someone who couldn't let him tell you he'd seen her there."

"Unless . . ."

I waited for him to finish it. He was thinking. He came out of his revery and he caught my questioning look.

"No," he said. "I'm wrong on that. I hadn't thought it through. This doesn't rule anybody out."

"Not even Patience?"

"I can't see how he could have had anything about last night that he could have tried to hold over her, but suppose last night wasn't her first visit? Suppose he'd seen her there other times. Suppose she and Thomas had a thing going."

"More likely," I said, "it would be that he heard the shot and he heard it after he saw Patience go into the house."

"A shot fired in that back room wouldn't be heard out in the street. When the precinct guys came riding their sirens, we were in a back room and we didn't hear a thing."

"I can't go for any Patience–Tommy affair," I said. "I know Patience Grimm, Schmitty, and you don't. They couldn't have been having a thing because Patience doesn't have things—and, for that matter, Tommy didn't either. He always married his. His promiscuity was consecutive, and even if he was breaking his pattern, it would never have been with Patience. You've seen Allegra and Louella. Wait till you see the others. Tommy didn't crave variety. He always wanted more of the same, and it was never anything like Patience Grimm."

"It's only a possibility," the inspector said as he slid the car into gear, "but it is a possibility. She may not look it, but she's human, and a lot of the time the ones who look it the least are the most human. They keep it locked up and it builds. This wouldn't be the first time it built to the combustion point."

"He didn't keep his locked up," I argued. "He married."

"So she was hot for it and he wasn't. A setup like that can drive a woman out of her mind, even without the guy making it even more unbearable by parading the goodies in front of her."

"And Allegra's alibi?" I asked.

"It's phony. You can bet on that, but you want to remember that it cuts six ways. It works equally well for all six of them."

"You're not thinking of a joint effort?"

The inspector shook his head.

"Too fancy," he said, "but if they've all been wanting to do it, they could be banding together to cover up for the one who finally had the guts to squeeze the trigger."

"So you really think it's one of the six?"

"I'm open. Any one of them is a possibility, but it doesn't have to be."

"If it isn't, then why the joint alibi?"

"They knew they'd be prime suspects. What should they do? Sit back in serene confidence that the truth will out and they'll be okay? Why not co-operate with the rest of the girls and get herself covered?"

"Even if each one of them is thinking that one of the others did it and that they're protecting a killer?"

"You know what they're thinking?" Schmitty said. "How about 'there but for the grace of God go I'? It makes them of a mind to help out."

"Unless it was one of them and she told the others," I said, "how could they know it had happened and in time to get organized on so complicated an alibi? I've been wondering about that. Doesn't it say something to you?"

"The Grimm woman called you. Do you think that's the only call she made?"

"Six calls and succeeding in reaching all of them? That

would be a busy evening even for as efficient a type as Patience."

"She had a lot of time," the inspector said, "and she didn't have to call all of them. It could have been just one —say, Allegra. Then that one could have rallied the sisterhood, and they'd get together to set the thing up."

He had, of course, been way ahead of me on the thinking. I've learned to expect that. There had been all those questions to Howard, the doorman, about Allegra having gone out and come back in again. It had seemed to me that the inspector had been casting the widest possible net and I'd had no notion of what he might have been after.

Now I was seeing the sense of it. Unless the six had actually been together and Patience, calling around, had located them at Louella's, then it did follow that they would all have had to have been home in time to be reached with Patience's warning. If it had been that way, it would have needed the most complicated and time-consuming round of phone calls back and forth to get all six of them set on the alibi story if at that point they hadn't gone out to meet somewhere and kick it around until they had it set up so that they would all be saying the same thing and all be letter-perfect in the story.

I still felt with the inspector that the alibi was about as valid as a Ruritanian doubloon, but it seemed as though there had to be some element of truth in it. They had been together for part of the evening, if only just long enough to work up the alibi and rehearse themselves in it. They might all be quick studies, but that hadn't been something that could have been done in a minute.

I shared my belated thinking with the inspector.

"Unless," I said, "they concocted the alibi in the afternoon at Dodo's and agreed on it in preparation for the main event."

"A conspiracy?" Schmitty muttered. "No. You can't make that one work out. It would have to be that one of them had an appointment with Thomas and was set to go there and kill him. Otherwise, it's too much preparation and taking too many people into her confidence on something that was too far from being sure. How could she know she was going to catch him at home that particular evening? How would she know she was going to be able to bring it off during that particular stretch of time? After it was done and she knew she'd accomplished it, yes. Before that, just on spec, no."

"There's something else," I said.

Now that I'd begun thinking, ideas were coming at me.

"What else?" the inspector asked.

"The typewriter and stuff, the way it was set out on display. That made sense for Allegra as long as we thought she was going to say: 'Yes, I killed him, but look at what he was doing to me and what he threatened to do. Where is a jury that will say I didn't have the right to defend myself?' It makes no sense if she hurried away to set up an alibi for herself. Why would she leave it all around or, more than that, set it out so that it would point to her?"

"She changed her mind," Schmitty said. "They claim women do that. I don't know that they do it any more than men, but I do know that killers do it all the time. She kills him and she plans on making those exhibits work in her defense. But once she's out of the house, she begins having second thoughts. She's worked up into a pretty good panic by then. Anyhow, if we believe that Patience did find the door unlocked, that might mean that the killer went out of there in a rush. The more she thinks about it, the less she feels like depending on an understanding jury. It was going to be a grandstand act and she'd liked the picture of herself doing it but, now that she's actually confronted with carrying it off, she has a loss of nerve. She goes for denial and the alibi instead."

"And even in the face of the evidence she'd set up, she wouldn't have been worrying about the dangers of changing horses in midstream?"

"What's to say she wasn't worrying? It worries her, but she has no choice. Her justifiable-homicide horse has drowned under her."

"The way she was with you last night? Would you call that a woman who'd lost her nerve?"

"That's a gal with plenty of bounce to her," Schmitty said. "It could be that she got that alibi organized, and she had so much confidence in it that she was riding high again. Even so, there was evidence of some loss of nerve. She told us those conflicting stories on how long she'd been asleep."

I nodded.

"Actually," I said, "unless you can bust that alibi open, Schmitty, they have something there that will knock over any jury. Who's going to believe that these six women could ever get together without any shred of animosity and build up such a loyalty one to the other that five of them would lie for the one? There aren't many people who won't say it's against nature and that therefore they must be telling the truth."

"Don't I know it?" the inspector groaned.

"There's another thing," I said. I was still thinking. "He came home. He undressed. His bell rang. He went downstairs naked—he'd do that even when he wasn't full of champagne. Come to think of it, he probably wasn't, because he didn't stay at the party long. He let her in and they went up as far as the living room, but they stopped and had it out there. She shot him and she never was up in the bedroom. She didn't know that all that evidence was laid out there against her."

"No good," Schmitty said. "Who laid it out and why?"

I persisted. "It was such an uncomfortable place for typing that we've been thinking that he couldn't have done it there, but what's to say he didn't? It would account for some of his typos. The way he typed, nothing could have made it comfortable. It's not impossible that he worked there."

"The dust says the stuff hadn't been there long," the inspector reminded me.

That objection wasn't stopping me.

"He came in," I said. "He had some idea of a follow-up on the game he played with the invitations. He undressed and he brought the stuff out to work on it. Before he got started, she rang the bell."

"No, Baggy," the inspector said. "You're not thinking."

"I thought at long last I was."

"You're not. There are too many things wrong with it. What was laid out? The typewriter? I'll come to that. Think about the pieces he'd cut off his stationery. What would he want with those? All they're good for is evidence that he wrote the anonymous letters. They were discarded stuff. Why would he have kept them in the first place? I'll come to that too. The invitations? What would he want with those? The party was over. There was no paper. There were no envelopes. There was nothing he could have been about to type on. All that stuff was put out for us to find. It could serve no other purpose. If Allegra never got above the living-room floor, then she can't be the killer."

"You said you'd come to the typewriter and those cut-off letter-paper tops," I reminded him.

"Yes," he said. "They're important. Think about them awhile."

I'd been so absorbed with all those great thoughts I'd had coming at me and with defending them against the inspector's skepticism, that I'd been taking no notice of where he'd been driving and where he'd stopped. When at that point he shoved his feet into his shoes, I thought to look around me. We were parked against the curb in front of the house where Tommy Thomas had died. The inspector's car was blocking the garage entrance, but Tommy, of course, was past making any objection to that.

"Something to look at here?" I asked.

"The body," Schmitty said. "The place where he died."

"Hasn't the body been removed yet?"

"Euclid's body."

"Here?"

"He lived here."

The inspector led the way, not into CHEZ NEFERTITTY but across the street to a building directly opposite. It was one of those modernized tenements where modernization means the installation of new bathrooms, new kitchens, window air conditioners, and exorbitant rents. The long-since-soured smell of decades of cooked cabbage still hangs in the halls. The rats and the roaches have not been dispossessed or relocated.

One flight up there was a patrolman stationed at the door of the rear flat. He made way for the inspector and we went in. Euclid was there, his body still lying where it had fallen. The room, even to me, spoke volumes. My first thought was how much it reminded me of Tommy Thomas's place across the street. This, too, had the look of containing everything a man could want.

Here, of course, everything was on a much smaller scale, but in its way it presented the same picture of total self-indulgence and damn-the-expense. There were book-shelves well stocked with books—sociology texts, but other books as well, including several of those high-priced jobs that come out in small editions because they sell almost exclusively to university libraries.

I looked into a couple of them. They weren't library copies. They weren't secondhand either. There was a superb stereo setup and a fortune in records and tapes. There was a bar and it was stocked with twelve-year-old scotch, bonded Bourbon, and V.S.O.P. cognac. The furniture was good and everything was in good condition.

Massage parlors are money-makers, but no great chunks of it go to the kid in the street who passes out the fliers. The inspector had sensed from the first that Euclid would be in the blackmail business, but this residence of the student-sybarite was visible evidence of it.

There was some destruction. A smashed bottle of that great scotch lay on the floor with its contents in a pool around it. Again it was visible evidence of what Inspector Schmidt had sensed: Euclid had been a moving target, in fact a target in swift and violent motion. He had tried to

counter the gun by flinging the bottle of whisky at his as-
sailant. The whisky had missed. I could see the place
where it had slammed against the wall and smashed.
There was broken plaster there and an area that was still
wet.

There was a bedroom, and in there the bed stood unmade. I noticed the bed linen. It was beautiful stuff. In
every respect Euclid had had expensive tastes and he had
indulged them.

He'd also had a cleaning woman who came in every
day. The cleaning woman had found the body. She was
sitting in the bedroom with her hands folded. She was
eying the unmade bed morosely. She had been told that
she must not touch anything, and it was easy to see that
she was the kind of conscientious soul for whom a bed
lying unmade would be a reproach. She was itching to get
at it.

"I've got my work to do," she complained. "And them
cops, they won't leave me do it, not even to scrub up the
bathroom and make the bed."

The inspector found some sympathetic words for her
and patiently explained the necessity for leaving everything as it was till his men had finished with it.

"I know," she said. "You call the police and you don't
touch nothing until they come. So they came. They seen
how everything is. What's to wait for now? They're taking
pictures. They want a picture it'll show how I ain't made
up the bed?"

"They're only doing their job," Schmitty told her.

She sniffed.

"Their job," she said. "I seen them. They're putting
chalk marks on the floor I'll have to clean off, and they're

squirting dust around like as if there ain't enough dusting to do without they go making more. They tell me it's for finding fingerprints, but I can tell you, you don't find nothing by putting stuff on it to cover it up."

Schmitty wasn't going to attempt to explain the finger-printing process to her. He left it with telling her that the men knew their job.

She sniffed again.

"They know their job," she said, "and nice Mr. Mallory, he never done nobody no hurt, he gets killed. They know their job and we're none of us safe."

"You found the body?" the inspector said.

"Who else? If it wasn't for me, he'd be laying there all day with nobody even to close the poor boy's eyes. They'll close his eyes, won't they?"

Assuring her on that point, the inspector pressed on. Detail by detail, he had to dig it out of her. It wasn't that she showed any reluctance to tell her story. It was just that she had difficulty keeping her mind on it. It kept straying to her worries. Were they going to cut nice Mr. Mallory up in one of them autopsies? And what would it hurt if they let her get a few nice flowers to put into the poor boy's hand?

She had come at her usual time, nine o'clock. She always came at that time when he would be off to school, except Saturdays when she came in the afternoon at one because he didn't go to school Saturdays and it was a day he could catch up on sleep which he needed, with all the studying and reading he did.

"Sundays I don't come in," she said.

"You have a key?"

"I have to have a key. This is New York. You can't go

leaving doors unlocked. Not even for a minute you can't. Look what happened to my other gentleman. They say he left the door unlocked and he was found dead in there with the door open. I can't think Mr. Mallory done like that, leaving his door open. He was a decent, sensible lad. He wasn't like that other one."

"Thomas across the street?" Schmitty asked.

"Yes, him. I always said he'd be sorry the way he was all the time going around the house with his clothes off. Now it's happened. He ain't even died decent with his pants on."

There were other such side excursions, but Inspector Schmidt stayed with her until he had from her everything she had to tell. She had worked for Tommy Thomas for many years. She went way back to before his first marriage. After some prodding and prying, the inspector pinned it down to the very beginning, when Tommy had first fixed the place up as bachelor quarters for himself. She had taken care of it for him from the first day. He'd never had any other cleaning woman.

She went in there every day and cleaned and dusted and did everything that needed doing. She had been in the day before. When Schmitty questioned her about the bedroom, she stoutly insisted that she had left it with never a speck of dust anywhere. She knew nothing about the typewriter or the stacks of paper. They hadn't been on the bedside cabinet when she had done up the bedroom. More than that, she had never seen any typewriter.

"He never had no typewriter in the house," she said. "Mr. Mallory, he's got a typewriter, but never Mr. Tommy. He was a different kind of gentleman."

The inspector explored that with her, but she insisted

that there had never been a typewriter on the premises. She couldn't have been more explicit about it or more definite. There had never been even the smallest nook or cranny in the house that had at any time not been open to her.

She explained that down through the years her work in the house had never been interrupted. Whether Tommy had been living there or not made little difference. Periods when he had been married and living elsewhere the work had, of course, been lighter, but the place had never been neglected. Six days a week she had been in there, even if it had been only to deal with the one day's deposit of New York dust.

At the times when he had been in residence, she had done his laundry and had taken care of his clothes, and periodically she had emptied closets. Similarly, she had been into all cupboards and bureau drawers, putting the clean laundry away where it belonged and at regular intervals putting in fresh shelf papers and drawer linings. If there had ever been a typewriter in the place, she would have seen it.

"He never wrote anything," she said. "He like dictated."

She explained that when Euclid Mallory wanted to leave her a message, she would find it typed out for her. He would leave it in the typewriter and, every morning when she came in, she would look there in case there might be a message or some instructions.

"Mr. Tommy," she said. "He always used that tape-recorder thing. Way back when I first worked for him he showed me how to work it. First thing, every day I came

in there, I'd push the playback button in case he left me
any message."

The last time she had been in the house, the morning of
the day before, there had been nothing on the tape.
Asked about the times when there was something on it
that had not been for her, she stoutly insisted that she
never listened to them if they weren't for her.

"How could you know they weren't for you if you
didn't listen?" the inspector asked.

"When he was talking to me, he started by saying my
name, Lottie. That's my name, Lottie. I turn it on and, if
it don't say Lottie right off, I don't listen. I switch it off.
I'm no nosy snoop."

When Schmitty questioned her about the last time she
had tried the tape recorder, she told him that then the
tape had been blank. It had, in fact, except for occasions
when he had left Lottie a message, been blank for a long
time.

"Since before he married his last one," she said.

For an old retainer she was curiously ignorant of
Tommy's private life, or she professed to be. She knew
none of his wives and she knew none of his friends. There
had been parties and there had at times been overnight
guests, but she knew of them only through the number of
used glasses that needed washing and ashtrays that
needed emptying and cleaning.

"I knew when there'd been somebody overnight," she
said, "because there'd be the beds to make up in the
other bedroom and the bed linen to change and the
towels and like that."

Mostly, during the times when she would be in there
working, the house had been empty. There had been oc-

casions when Tommy himself had been there. It was from those times that she had known of his penchant for nakedness, but there had never been anyone else.

"He wouldn't stay naked when I was there," she said. "I had that out with him at the beginning. I told him I wouldn't work for him if he done that. He'd come into a room and see I was there, he'd back right out again and put him some pants on."

The inspector asked her how long she had been working for Mallory. She put it at about three months.

"How did you get this job?" the inspector asked. "Did they know each other?"

"Mr. Tommy and Mr. Mallory? No. Mr. Euclid here, he seen me working across the street, and one day he stopped me when I was coming out over there and he asked me could I give him like an hour a day."

"Did he ever ask you questions about Mr. Thomas? You know, try to get you to give him some gossip about him or anything like that?"

"He was always asking questions about Mr. Tommy, but it wasn't anything wrong. It was what he was studying in college. They study that, how people live, different kinds of people and the different ways they live. That's what he was studying. They call it sociology."

IX

There was nobody else available for questioning, nobody who might have seen someone come or go, and nobody who might have heard the shots. Those converted tenements house no families: they are tenanted by singles or by young couples, both of whom go out to work. From eight-thirty in the morning till after five in the evening on weekdays, such buildings are empty. Occasionally, of course, one of the tenants might be home ill or between jobs or taking a day off for one reason or another, but on that morning there had been nobody in the building. Here and there you might find a night worker or somebody who worked odd hours, but in this building there had been only one of those, Euclid Mallory himself.

"Of course," Inspector Schmidt said, "that's the way it would be."

He was putting his shoes back on. Lottie had eyed him sharply when he had shucked out of them right after settling in to question her. On the basis of her experience with Tommy Thomas, she had been about to protest, but since Schmitty stopped with the shoes, she had relaxed.

"You can't be lucky all the time," I said.

We went out of there and, when we were away from Lottie, the inspector told me that he hadn't been bewailing his luck. He was satisfied that he had a clear picture of the killing and of the events that led up to it.

"Euclid had the perfect setup for blackmail, a place where at the right time of day people could come and go unobserved. The suckers are more likely to make a payoff if they can feel sure there's only one blackmailer they're going to have to buy. Euclid saw someone last night. He called the killer and set it up for this morning. The killer was to come to his place sometime a little after eight-thirty and they would make a deal."

"He may have thought it a good setup for him," I said. "He should have recognized that it was an even better setup for the killer."

"Yes," the inspector agreed. "That was his mistake, but it was an understandable mistake."

"Not as smart as he thought he was."

"I wouldn't say that. I'd say he was led astray by his experience."

The inspector drew me the whole picture. The little flat was full of expensive things, and the source of such plenty was obvious. Blackmail hadn't been any new game for Euclid Mallory. He had been an old hand at it and he had been a highly successful practitioner.

"Husbands whose wives had to be kept in ignorance," Schmitty said. "Politicians with an image that had to be preserved, and even plain, solid citizens who were ashamed of where they went and who would pay and pay rather than have it generally known—he knew those types well. They were sheep for the shearing. It would never enter his head that he had to be afraid of anybody like that."

"Killers are different," I said. "There's always someone

who can't be pushed or who is pushed too far and turns. This was someone who had already turned. Euclid should have thought of that."

"You can see why he didn't," Schmitty said. "The word on these massage parlors is that there has been increasing mob infiltration in the business. In his job you can figure he was coming up against two kinds of people—the victim types he could push around, and the mob types who were too dangerous to monkey with. He was faced with such a black-and-white situation day after day that he just stopped seeing individuals. Respectable citizens were easy prey. The mob? Look out, brother."

"And women?" I asked.

"The odds are that he had no experience with blackmailing women," Schmitty said. "On his job there wouldn't be much opportunity for that."

"So he made the mistake of thinking a woman would be like a man?" I said.

"There are two mistakes you can make about women: one is thinking they'll be just like men, and the other is thinking they'll be nothing like men. Anyhow, we've got this thing narrowed down a little."

"To a respectable type who's not afraid to kill?"

"Better than that. We can eliminate Louella Thomas."

"Of the six, she was always the least likely," I said. "She'd been Tommy's first. She'd had the longest time to cool down. She'd gone the longest without doing anything about him. Why would she erupt now?"

"Taking it another way," the inspector said, "she was the one of the six with the best right to feel she'd been injured. All the others could have had mixed feelings. They could have blamed themselves some. Actually, they should have. It wasn't like they hadn't had some warning. She'd had none."

"And what eliminates her now?"

"Euclid's killing is a result of Thomas's killing. We're settling for that, aren't we?"

"It's the most likely assumption."

"It sure is. So if we say that Euclid saw Thomas's killer and made a try at blackmail, then we must say there's one killer for the two jobs. Since Louella couldn't have done Euclid, she didn't do Thomas."

"It follows," I agreed. "But what's to say she couldn't do Euclid?"

"*We're* to say, you and I. She's alibied for the Mallory killing, and the two of us are her alibi witnesses."

The morning's program, until it had been interrupted and revised by the news of the Euclid Mallory killing, had been to continue the round of the Thomas ex-wives. Now it occurred to me that the first order of business might be to go back to Allegra Thomas to check on how well she might be doing for a morning alibi.

Inspector Schmidt, however, took off on a course that would bring him nowhere near Allegra's apartment. I asked him why.

"Waste of time," he said. "If she's thinking she'll need a morning alibi, she'll have one set up with the doorman who's working the morning shift. On what we've got now, the first thing I want to know about is typewriters."

"Oh, yes. Lottie never saw one."

"And I'm putting my money on Lottie," the inspector said. "She's the first unquestionably honest and reliable witness I've had on this thing—the first except for you,

Baggy, and at noticing details and remembering them she's a lot better than you."

"It's the intrinsic quality of the small mind," I said. "Little minds pick up on little things and they hang on to them."

"On an investigation," Schmitty said, "give me the little minds anytime. I don't need the heavy thinkers. I'll take care of that department myself."

"You're good both ways," I said. "You pick up on the little things as well."

"That's just training and experience," Schmitty said.

It wasn't modesty. Inspector Schmidt is a man who knows his worth. He won't overestimate himself, but no more will he underestimate himself.

Our next port of call was the Madison Avenue offices of Thomas & Adams. En route the inspector worked his phone. He had his men out on various lines of the investigation and he was keeping in touch, staying abreast of anything that might be reported in. After listening for a considerable time and saying not enough to give me much lead on what he was picking up, he turned and filled me in.

"We were going to ask about typewriters," he said. "Now it's going to be typewriters and party invitations. One of the boys has located the print shop that did a quick, special rush job on them. They were given a sample and for a price they made copies to meet a rush deadline. The print shop justifies the price because on a rush order like that they had to pay a lot of overtime. Since the customer was ready to pay whatever they asked, they took on the job."

"Who was the customer?"

"The order came from the Thomas & Adams office."

"So what else is new? It was Tommy's game. We know that. Okay. Lottie never saw the typewriter, so maybe he never kept it in the house, but it was there last night."

"It isn't the print shop that does the Thomas & Adams work. This outfit never had an order from them before. That was another reason for them to take the job on. The printer figured that the outfit that had been getting the Thomas & Adams business maybe wasn't geared to handle this kind of a rush job and had turned it down. A more obliging and flexible print shop might be in line to pick up the whole Thomas & Adams account. That would be all future Thomas & Adams printing and engraving."

"Who put in the order?"

"A man called and identified himself as Thomas. The deal was made over the phone. A messenger brought the sample invitation and a messenger came to pick the order up. He came with an envelope. It was cash payment on delivery. That surprised the printer a bit. He had assumed he would be billing Thomas & Adams for it."

"It wasn't office business, and Tommy's pockets were always full of cash."

"Yeah," Schmitty said. "The guy was a character. He was always carrying cash except for a lot of the time when he didn't have a pocket to carry it in."

The offices were small, but they were unmistakably in the Tommy Thomas manner—handsome, elegant, expensive. If the Vernon Adams touch showed anywhere in them, it could only have been in the choice of office machinery. There were no old, beat-up typewriters.

Thomas & Adams held the patents on some small component that no computer can do without. They licensed computer manufacturers all over the world to make the thing and incorporate it in their computers. They did no manufacturing of their own; they just collected the royalties. The story was that Vernon Adams had had the opportunity to buy up the patents and nothing to buy them with. Tommy Thomas had supplied the capital.

Wall Street types, who knew about such things, always said that Tommy had done well. His share of the firm income had been a handsome return on the money he'd put into it, even though it had been only a minor part of the total Thomas income. For Vernon Adams, however, his equal share of the Thomas & Adams take had lifted him from a level of decent affluence to one of substantial wealth.

That, of course, looks like a good deal for Vernon Adams and nothing of much importance for Tommy Thomas, but the office also handled all of Tommy's investments for him; and I didn't need to be told by the Wall Street types that it meant that it was the Vernon Adams brains and the Vernon Adams energy that year after year had been making Tommy richer. The only thing Tommy Thomas had ever known about money was how to spend it. Some of the Wall Street types, more addicted to making than to spending, will tell you that all he ever knew about money was how to throw it away. I make no such judgments. One man's necessity may well be another man's extravagance.

It wasn't a heavily populated office. There was an outer room complete with glossy receptionist. There was a secretary who shared an office with a stenographer. A bookkeeper and her assistant shared another office. There was an office for Vernon Adams and an office for Tommy Thomas. That last one had never been much used.

The inspector asked for Adams, and the receptionist hit a desk intercom to give the secretary our names. The relaying of communication to Adams must have been instantaneous, because in no time at all he was with us in the reception area, coming with both hands outstretched to grab mine.

"George," he said, "he liked you. He liked you very much. It bothered him that he never read your books because he liked you so much, but you know how Tommy was."

I've never known what accepted business practice might be. How far does a man go in mourning for a dead partner? Vernon had gone all the way—black suit, white shirt, black knit tie, black-rimmed white handkerchief in his breast pocket, and red-rimmed eyes in his face.

Except for the red-rimmed eyes, he reminded me of John Gielgud in a production of *The Importance of Being Earnest* I had seen years before. Whether it had been the stage lighting or some special dye that could have been called nothing but Lugubrious Black, the Gielgud mourning had been blacker than anything seen by man before or since. However it had been done, Vernon Adams was now close to matching it.

We went through the routine. It was a terrible thing. Tommy had been such a great fellow, more like a brother than a partner, really like a madcap younger brother Vernon had been taking care of. He catalogued Tommy's virtues and, when he ran out of those, he catalogued Tommy's faults, extolling them into virtues.

"I could imagine him getting into all kinds of trouble,"

he said. "But he was so big and so strong and so quick, it always seemed as though he could take care of himself."

"Nobody's so big and strong that a well-placed bullet won't bring him down," Schmitty said.

"Yes, Inspector, I know. I'm glad you came around with George. You're just the man I wanted to see."

"You have something to tell me?"

"Something to ask of you."

He was fretting about the funeral arrangements. Could the inspector tell him how soon the body would be released for burial? Vernon would be doing the funeral arrangements. After all, there was nobody else—no wife, no relatives.

"No sitting wife," Schmitty said.

Vernon didn't like the comment. He winced just perceptibly, but he quickly adjusted his expression and asked if the inspector couldn't do something to expedite the release of the body.

Schmitty assured him that it wouldn't be long.

"There are some questions I am hoping you can answer," Schmitty said.

Adams cast a quick glance in the direction of the receptionist.

"Let's take this into my office," he suggested. "We'll be more comfortable in there."

"Thanks," the inspector said. "I'd like to get off my feet."

Ushered into Vernon's office, the inspector did more than get off his feet. He shucked out of his shoes. Vernon worked at not noticing. He had been Tommy's partner— he should have been able to take it in stride. I caught myself wondering whether Tommy had ever put in any office time with his clothes off.

"Inspector," Vernon said, "I hope you understand that I am in a most delicate position. I know nothing and I can't deal in conjecture. There are things a man cannot permit himself to think about his friends."

"The man is dead. There's nothing that could be said against him now that can hurt him in any way."

"Tarnishing his memory, Inspector? I wasn't thinking anything like that. There was never anything anyone could have said against Tommy."

"Then you weren't worrying about questions I might be asking you about him?"

"No, Inspector."

"Don't you want to see his murderer caught?"

"This may shock you, Inspector, but it would please me most if we could just let Tommy rest in peace."

"I'm in no position to do that, Mr. Adams. I have my official duty."

"Yes, but so many murders do remain unsolved. Could one more make a difference?"

"The ones that go unsolved are the ones that are not capable of solution. It's not because we don't try."

"If all of us who knew Tommy were to agree to let bygones be bygones, then it would be incapable of solution, wouldn't it?"

"More difficult," the inspector said. "I hope it would not be impossible."

"I hope you will not hold it too bitterly against me, Inspector, if I make your work as difficult as I can."

"I'm used to that, Mr. Adams," Schmitty said. "It's par for the course."

"You won't get back at me by delaying release of the body?" Adams asked.

"That's not the way I work."

Adams rose. He was tacitly inviting the inspector to climb back into his shoes and leave.

"Sit down, Mr. Adams," Schmitty said. "I have yet to ask my questions. You may even find there are some you are prepared to answer."

Reluctantly Adams sat.

"Fire away, Inspector," he said.

"How's business?" Schmitty began.

Having been braced for something quite different, Adams relaxed visibly.

"As always," he said. "We can't complain. In this business 'as always' is good. We're not subject to any great fluctuations. The securities market has been sluggish for a considerable time, but that has no effect on us. We have never been in any speculative situation."

"Mr. Thomas had an old typewriter."

"Oh, that. I suppose there's never been another man in this world who could be sentimentally attached to a decrepit wreck of an old portable. The thing hadn't been properly operable for years and years, but he hung on to it. When it finally became hopeless and he had to dump it, I really think that parting with it upset him more than any of his divorces."

"You say he dumped it?"

"Yes. It was an ancient model nobody had seen for years. The manufacturer had gone out of business. To repair it, the repair man would have had to scour the country for other wrecks of the same model in the hope that he might be able to cannibalize them for the parts he would have needed to do a repair."

"When you say he dumped it, did you see it go out?"

"I know this is all about that prank with the party invitations," Vernon said.

He was being the serious citizen, impatient of silly frivolities.

"And the threatening letters addressed to his sixth wife," the inspector added.

"If all the letters were like the one I saw, they were so outrageously far out that nobody could take them seriously. All that was just a crude joke, and Tommy had nothing to do with it. Just because they were badly typed on an old typewriter with dirty keys meant nothing. His wasn't the only old, dirty typewriter in the world, and he wasn't the only sloppy typist. Anyhow he no longer had the typewriter, so that's out."

"You haven't answered my question."

"What was your question, Inspector?"

"Did you see that old typewriter go out?"

"I gave it to Selma and told her to get rid of it. Selma is Mrs. Mirsky, our receptionist. When we shut up for the evening, Selma left it on her desk with a note on it. The note was for the cleaning women who do the building at night. It told them to remove the machine and get rid of it. We do that with things of this sort. A cleaning woman can take it to a junkman and she might get fifty cents for it."

We had Mrs. Mirsky in and we had the secretary in. They had a clear recollection of the day the old typewriter went out. They remembered it because Mr. Adams had told them how cut up Mr. Thomas was over parting with it.

It had been done exactly as Adams said, left for the cleaning women to remove. The next morning it hadn't been there.

"You had it on your desk with a note of instructions?" the inspector asked Mrs. Mirsky. "Were you the last to leave the office that night?"

She wasn't certain. She couldn't remember. The secretary took her off the hook.

"I was the last to leave that night," she said. "I locked up."

Was she certain of it? She was. She explained that the stenographer was new. It had been another girl at the time the inspector was asking about. They had been the last to leave the office and the secretary had had the responsibility of locking up. She remembered because she had been annoyed when the stenographer had stopped to check out the old typewriter.

"She had an idea that she might take it and have it repaired to give to her kid brother who needed one for school," the secretary explained. "I told her it was beyond repair. The shift lock was gone and the machine wouldn't line space. You had to turn the roller by hand, and it had just about everything else wrong with it. But she had to see for herself, and I was trying to get her out of here so I could lock up."

"So it was on the desk when you locked up that night, and it was gone in the morning."

"Yes. The note instructed them to take it away and get rid of it."

"But they didn't," Schmitty said.

"It wasn't here in the morning."

"It's sitting on the bedside stand in Mr. Thomas's bedroom. It was there when we found the body last night."

Adams smiled one of those sad little smiles.

"The soppy old rascal," he said. "He yessed me all the way and then he snuck back here after we were all gone and rescued it. Just think of that."

"I have been thinking of it," Schmitty said.

He moved on to the order for the duplication of Dodo's invitation. Nobody knew anything about that, but then the secretary thought of something.

"Yes, yes, yes," she said. "That will be the crazy call we got. I thought it was some stupid new way of soliciting business, and the man was so downright rude I just hung up on him."

The inspector wanted more detail and she supplied it. Some printer had called and asked whether the invitations had been satisfactory and started a spiel about being available for any kind of printing and engraving work. The secretary told him that he must have the wrong number. He asked if it was Thomas & Adams and, when she said it was but he'd never done any work for them, the man became abusive, and the secretary hung up on him.

"The silly old rascal," Adams murmured.

I'd heard just such a fondly amused tone used for the antics of a pet dog.

The secretary was shaking her head. She was still not satisfied about the typewriter.

"The machine was here when I locked up and it was gone when I opened the office the following morning," she said. "How could Mr. Thomas get in? He had no key."

"The night watchman would let him in," Mrs. Mirsky suggested. "Or if he came back when the cleaning women were in here, they might have let him in."

"He had a key," Adams said.

"Oh, no, Mr. Adams," the secretary insisted. "Don't you remember? He lost his keys and we were about to have the lock cylinder changed, but he had only mislaid them and he found them again before we'd had it done. Don't you remember he insisted on taking the office key off his key holder and leaving it with you. He said he never came in out of hours anyhow and it was a responsibility he didn't need. He insisted on it."

Adams gave her a condescending look. It was also a look of curbed irritation. He was a man who was stretching his patience to cover a great deal of nonsense, and in a time of mourning when he was in no mood for it.

"Of course, I remember," he said. "You may think you are privy to everything that goes on in this office, but you are not. I didn't take the key. He was insistent, but I was more insistent. It would have been ridiculous his not having an office key. If something happened to me and it was on a weekend when you wouldn't be available and he would have to get in here for some necessary papers, we would have been in a sorry fix."

"Oh," the secretary said. "I didn't know."

"That's all right."

The woman had been put in her place. It was time to be generous.

"What are your hours here?" Schmitty asked.

They were comfortable hours, nine-thirty to four-thirty. It was a relaxed office.

Schmitty thanked them and went back inside to retrieve his shoes. I remained out in the reception area with Vernon. He whispered to me.

"If that's all he wants," he said, "am I relieved! I thought sure he was going to try to get me to throw poor Allegra to the wolves. I wouldn't want to be the one to do that. Of course, Allegra shouldn't have done it, but I can see where Tommy drove her to it. Those letters. I can't think what got into him. I've been thinking maybe he was going out of his mind."

The inspector thanked them again and we pulled out. He seemed well-satisfied with what he had picked up in the office, even though I couldn't see that it added much. I told him what I was thinking and I also told him what Vernon Adams had whispered to me.

Schmitty shrugged it off.

"Is that what he thinks, or is it what he knows? I get too much of what people think and not nearly enough of what they know. What they think they can keep to themselves."

We grabbed the usual bad sandwich and the worse cup of coffee at a Madison Avenue lunch counter before we picked up again where we'd left off that morning on the Mrs. Thomases. Charlotte was next on the inspector's list. She received us out on her terrace where she was doing something esoterically horticultural with the tree roses she had growing out there. She was wearing the much-talked-of hat. It was her gardening hat. She took it off long enough to show us that frequently quoted label inside.

"Well, Inspector," she said, taking a brisk tone with him, "when may we expect you to put a stop to all this horrid killing?"

"I'm doing my best, Mrs. Thomas."

"And you're about to say that we're not being any help. If you are going to say it, it'll be unjust, since you know that our ridiculous little fable did no harm."

"What ridiculous little fable, Mrs. Thomas?"

"Oh, take your shoes off," she said. "I know you want to. I read all of dear George's books, so I know more than a little about you, Inspector. Don't tell me that you even for a moment believed that nonsense about the six of us getting together for the whole evening to stuff ourselves with more of the very things that Dodo had given us and all to organize our own little Veterans of Domestic Wars."

"No," Schmitty said. "I never believed it. Now, would you like to tell me why you've given up on it?"

"I can't say I ever had much faith in its being any good, but I didn't mind going along with the rest of Tommy's relicts. Now that it has become unnecessary—or would the word be redundant, George? You know about those things—why go on with it?"

"How unnecessary?" Schmitty asked.

"That boy across the street from Tommy's—Allegra couldn't have done him and, since someone has her gun and has killed both of them, then if the second one can't be Allegra's doing, it follows as the night the day—isn't that Shakespeare, George?—that the first one can't have been hers either. She's as innocent as a newborn babe, and maybe innocenter."

"She's got herself an even better alibi for this morning?"

"Then you haven't heard, Inspector? After you left her last night, she quite went to pieces. Hysterics. Screaming hysterics. She phoned her doctor. The way she screamed

over the phone, she scared him right into his britches and
into an absolutely unheard of house call. He took her
right over to New York Hospital, the Payne Whitney part,
you know. It isn't a padded cell but it's the nearest thing
to it that money can buy and strong-armed nurses never
for a moment letting Allegra out of their sight."

"That eliminates two of you. We were with the first
Mrs. Thomas at the time of this morning's murder. What
about you and the other three? How are you fixed for
alibis?"

Charlotte laughed.

"The rest of us, Inspector? Tommy was ancient history
for us, and anyhow he was really a cuddly bear when you
weren't married to him. It was all for Allegra because
she'd had those horrible letters and her gun had been
stolen."

"You knew it was her gun that had been used?"

"We knew Tommy had been shot. Patience called
Dodo as soon as she found the body, and Dodo called
Allegra and told her, and Allegra went looking in her bag
for her gun and it was gone, so she called Louella. She
picked Louella because she was his first. Not that it
makes her our leader or anything like that, but Allegra
felt easiest with her because she was the farthest away in
Tommy's life."

"And then you got together and cooked up the alibi?"

"Louella called the rest of us and got us together at her
house because, being a house and not an apartment, it
would be the best for privacy. We'd all had dinner by
that time and we'd all had different things, so it seemed
as though we'd be surest to remember something we'd re-

ally had even though it'd been at Dodo's and not for dinner."

"That was obvious," Schmitty said.

"I was afraid it might be," Charlotte murmured. "I'm glad I didn't have to go on with it to the place where I'd have had to tell you what we ate at Louella's. To say that I'd eaten all that gop twice in one day, back to back, would have made me upchuck. And your question, Inspector: if I'd ever considered killing anyone, it wouldn't have been with a gun. It would have been poison. This stuff I'm putting on the plants is nicotine. It kills bugs, but it has the same effect on people."

X

Before we left Charlotte, Inspector Schmidt did question her about her movements of the previous evening and of that morning. She had an alibi of sorts. From Dodo's party she had gone to her own place, planning to spend a quiet evening at home.

"I had George's new book," she said.

She had no more than started on the book when Dodo called her with the news about Tommy. The rest of the evening had gone to the get-together at Louella's of what she called the Veterans of Domestic Wars. In the morning she had slept late and had since been giving the day to horticulture on her terrace. The inspector could check it out with the building employees and with some of her fellow tenants.

"Several have been complaining today about my overenthusiastic watering," she said. "It came down on their windows. I just never can remember that there are all those people down below."

Agnes, Claire, and Constance remained to be questioned, but now that the six had backed away from their concocted alibi, Schmitty no longer felt that he had to question the remaining three himself. He delegated that to some of his men, and he didn't even bother to question the doorman in Charlotte's building.

"A waste of time," he said. "You know what I got out of Howard. If these women are lying, they'll get the guys who work the doors to back them up on it."

We went around to the hospital to see Allegra. She was calm and, apart from being unwontedly subdued, she seemed completely herself. Her doctor made no objections to the inspector's talking to her, warning only that he must not upset her.

"The nurse will be there," the doctor said. "If Mrs. Thomas shows even the slightest sign of agitation, you'll be right out on your ass, Inspector. I've worked with this nurse before. I know her potential. Don't kid yourself that she can't handle you."

"I'll be good," Schmitty promised.

"I'm consenting to your visit," the doctor explained, "only because Mrs. Thomas has been asking for you and she did get agitated when I tried to suggest to her that it might better wait."

It was an opening and the inspector took advantage of it.

"You wanted to see me, Mrs. Thomas," he began.

"Yes, Inspector. Thank you for coming. I do appreciate it."

"Don't give it a thought," Schmitty said, taking a comfortable chair and shedding his shoes. "Calling on the sick, that's a thing I do."

"And I am sick, Inspector. I'm sick with guilt."

"Guilt? What are you guilty of?"

"After you left me last night, Inspector, it hit me. It hit me hard."

She told us what hit her. Even though she had not herself pulled the trigger, she was seeing herself as quite as guilty of Tommy's murder as if she had.

"My gun was gone," she said. "Someone had stolen it and used it to kill Tommy, and I had set the stage. I tried to tell myself that I hadn't made it happen. It would have been done anyhow with some other gun and some other evidence to point to someone else, just as the evidence being used pointed to me."

She'd had a not unreasonable argument there, but she hadn't been able to convince herself with it.

"I was lying to you," she said. "I had half the world lying for me. Tommy was dead and it was my fault and I was making it worse by not being honest with you. I knew I couldn't go on with it. I was going to have to tell you the truth, and at the same time I was afraid. I went to pieces."

"Since I never believed it, Mrs. Thomas, that alibi didn't matter too much."

"But there is my gun and I was careless with it. I let someone steal it and now it isn't only Tommy. It's that poor, innocent child as well."

"What child?"

For a moment she had the inspector confused.

"The boy across the street from Tommy's, the one who was murdered this morning, murdered with my gun."

"Your gun? We've no way of knowing that until we find your gun, and we won't even know if the two of them were killed with the same gun till we've had the slugs out and our ballistics people have reported on the comparison of the bullets."

"I'm no fool, Inspector, even though I do behave like one. You're talking about absolute proof, but think of all

the times you've known things before they were proven.
Anyhow, first it was Tommy and now that unfortunate
child and no telling where it will stop. Someone has my
gun and is going around killing with it, killing indiscriminately."

"Not indiscriminately," the inspector said. "Euclid
Mallory was no child. He was a fully grown man and he'd
been having a highly successful career as a blackmailer.
That's a dangerous trade. The hazards caught up with
him."

"My gun did the catching up," Allegra said, "and I
don't like that."

"We're working on it," Schmitty told her. "Do you
know anything that could help us?"

"*Cherchez la femme,*" Allegra said.

I assumed that she was suggesting one of the other five.
I was thinking that loyalty to the Veterans of Domestic
Wars might never have weighed too heavily with Allegra.
It had been useful to her as long as she had been the
prime suspect, but now that she was in the clear, it ap-
peared to be no longer operative.

"Opportunity to swipe your gun?" Schmitty asked. "Or
something more that you know about one of the other ex-
wives? Be as specific as you can, Mrs. Thomas."

The question startled her.

"Tommy's other exes?" she said. "Oh, none of them.
Anyone who was at Dodo's party could have taken the
gun, even George here." She turned to me. "If it weren't
for the fact that it has been used," she said, "I would
have been sure you'd taken it."

"Me?" I said. "Why me?"

"Because you were the one who was upset by my having it. You disapproved. I would have guessed that you'd taken it to hand it over to the police because you'd told me that I should and I wasn't going to. Of course, since I didn't miss it until I went to look for it in my bag when Dodo told me Tommy had been shot, I never got around to thinking that, because obviously you wouldn't shoot Tommy."

"If you didn't think it then," I asked, "why bring it up now?"

I was annoyed and I was showing it. The nurse took a step toward me. It looked as though I might be about to be tossed out on my ass. Allegra, however, took it calmly, and the nurse stepped back and relaxed.

"I'm just trying to make the inspector understand that it could have been anyone."

"A woman who wasn't one of his exes?" the inspector said. "Come on, let's not play riddles."

"I don't know who," Allegra said. "I'd be rushing to tell you if I knew. It's just that for anyone who knew Tommy it stands to reason."

She laid out her reasoning for us. She had divorced Tommy. She had been out of his life. Since it was Tommy, that would mean he had been on his way into another marriage. It was the way he had always been.

The inspector laughed.

"You think that some gal, knowing his record, was so terrified of being married to him that she tried to escape by killing him before he could put the ring on her finger?"

"You think I'm an idiot and I don't blame you. You have every reason for thinking it."

"I don't think you're an idiot," Schmitty said. "I think you're still talking in riddles."

"He was Tommy and he hadn't changed. Going through it five times, he'd never changed; he wouldn't have changed now. I was gone. He was certainly looking around for a replacement. Suppose he's been considering several women, making his choice among them. Now suppose he's made up his mind. The way I see it, it was someone who was runner-up to me and now it's happened again. She's runner-up to someone else and she flips. She hasn't forgiven me and she's fed up with Tommy. Wouldn't she kill him maybe and try to rig it so I'd pay the penalty?"

"Then she might still be gunning for the gal who beat her out this second time," I said.

It seemed too far-fetched.

Inspector Schmidt shook his head. He wasn't thinking about how it seemed. He was thinking hard evidence.

"So far as we can tell," he said, "he wasn't seeing anybody."

"Tommy? That's impossible. What makes you think that? It can only be because you didn't know him. It's just too unlike Tommy."

"Before your divorce was there anyone?" Schmitty asked.

"No, of course not. That was never Tommy's way. It was only after a marriage had gone sour and he was back in that stable of his that he'd start looking around. Then he broke out the old typewriter and the tape recorder and started a fresh campaign. He never did it any other way."

"That's the point," the inspector said. "We have evidence that indicates that this time he didn't start any fresh campaign."

He told her about Lottie and the instructions on the tape recorder.

"She is definite about it," he said. "Since Thomas moved back, she's never once flipped the playback switch and brought in anything that wasn't a message to her."

Allegra wasn't ready to accept that. She argued that any love message he had recorded on tape would always have been removed from the machine and the tape sent to the lady he was courting.

"It's ridiculous to think he would just leave the tape sitting in the machine for his cleaning woman to tune in on it."

"You're assuming he would record the whole of one of his tapes in a single sitting," Schmitty said. "The times Lottie tuned in on one it must have been an unfinished job he left in the machine to come back to it later and finish it."

She was reluctant to give up on her theory.

"This time, then, there just hadn't been any that he'd left unfinished overnight," she insisted. "It doesn't mean there weren't any."

"Tell me something," Schmitty said. "Was Thomas your first husband?"

"My one and only," she answered. "Maybe I'll try it again one day, but the way I feel now, I don't think so."

"None of the others have married again," Schmitty remarked.

"Yes," she said. "We talked some about that. We were wondering whether there was something special about marriage to Tommy that left all of us with this once-is-enough-and-more-than-enough feeling, or if it is that we all just happen to be of a type that isn't built to do it more than once. It's been the same for all of us. Tommy was our first, and for all of us just the one marriage seems to have been a permanent cure. It's funny."

"Maybe it's sad," the inspector said.

"I don't know," Allegra murmured. "The sad one is Vernon. Has anyone talked to him since?"

"We saw him this morning," Schmitty said.

"He seemed very much as he's always been," I said. "Efficient and pompous. He's fussing about the funeral arrangements."

"Yes," Allegra said. "He'll have those. They will be something to occupy him. After the funeral is when it will hit him. He's the big loser. With Tommy gone, he has nobody. He hasn't even had time to get over the shock of losing Marian, and Vernon isn't another Tommy. What's that old line? No use running after a bus or a woman, there's always another one coming along. That was Tommy, but Vernon runs after buses. He takes his losses hard."

"His wife die?" Schmitty asked.

It was a reasonable question when one considered Vernon's ultra-black mourning.

"No. She left him. It's been almost a month now. She's filed for divorce."

"Yesterday at Dodo's he seemed to be bearing up," I said.

"Yesterday," Allegra said, "I was a bitch. You saw how hard it hit him when I made that totally unnecessary crack about Marian."

We pulled away from the hospital to keep an appointment the inspector had made with Tommy's lawyer. Tommy's will had been pulled out of the files and the lawyer was prepared to fill the inspector in on its terms.

"Eventually," the lawyer said, "almost everything will go to the Thomas Foundation."

He explained that the foundation had been established by Tommy's father and that during his lifetime Tommy had contributed heavily to it. The income from the foundation contributed to a wide and varying range of educational, cultural, and charitable organizations, with the foundation board deciding each year where the money might be most needed.

The inspector listened to the explanation but it was evident that he wasn't much interested. At his first opportunity he came in with a question.

"You said 'eventually.'" He asked, "When is 'eventually'? And what is the story till then?"

"Specific bequests," the lawyer said, "are minor—a watch, some cufflinks, studs, personal possessions, mementos going to friends." He paused and turned to me. "You're in there for something, Mr. Bagby. Some Waterford decanters, I believe."

At one of his parties I remembered admiring the decanters. Tommy evidently had also remembered.

"Nothing there anyone would kill him for," Schmitty said.

"Nothing in the will as a whole, Inspector. You asked about 'eventually.' Except for these bequests of personal possessions, everything goes into a trust. Out of the income of the trust the executors are to pay what amounts to a lifetime pension to a woman named Lottie Smith. She's been his maid and she will continue to receive wages at her current scale and will need to perform no services for the money. Similarly, there are to be monthly payments to his former wives equal to the monthly alimony payments they have been receiving. These payments are also to continue throughout their lives regardless of whether they remarry or not. Upon the death of the last of these seven, the six wives and the maid, the trust is to be dissolved and the principle will go to the Thomas Foundation. Also during the life of the trust all surplus income goes to the foundation. The executors are Vernon Adams and myself."

"He changed his will often," the inspector said.

"Whenever changing circumstances required an alteration."

"Each time he married, each time he was divorced?"

"Yes, Inspector, necessarily. During all his marriages the will read differently. Essentially there were two wills —one that he kept in force during his marriages, and one in the present form that was in force between marriages. In the other will that residual income that now goes to the Thomas Foundation went to his widow throughout her lifetime."

"Would you say that his wives knew the terms of his will?"

"I'm certain they did. Mr. Thomas had an extraordinarily open nature. He kept no secrets. He held back nothing. I've always thought that may have been one of the reasons why his marriages did not succeed. There is such a thing as too much candor. It can make life difficult."

"So a wife who wanted to be rid of him even to the point of killing him would have known that it was much to her advantage to do it before the divorce rather than after?"

"She would need to be an inordinately greedy woman, Inspector. His divorce settlements and alimony payments have always been extravagantly generous. Again and again I recommended to him that much less would be more than adequate."

"That didn't give you much," I told the inspector when we were clear of the lawyer's office.

"It didn't give me anything and I didn't expect it to," Schmitty said. "I had to touch all bases before I moved. I don't like to make an arrest and then have something new come up and hit me in the eye."

"You're ready to move?" I asked.

"I would have been ready a lot sooner if you'd told me everything you knew."

"Me? What didn't I tell you?"

Schmitty laughed.

"You held out on me," he said. "Now I'm holding out on you. You can try to figure it out while you're waiting. You know everything I know."

We were in his car and he was on the phone again. His office didn't have anything much for him, only the ballistics report on the comparison of the bullets taken from Euclid's body with the one taken out of Tommy's. That was as expected: the shot that killed Tommy Thomas and the ones that silenced Euclid Mallory had been fired out of the same gun and they were of a caliber that would have fitted the gun Allegra had handled so carelessly the previous afternoon at Dodo Baines's extravagant bash.

We returned to the Thomas & Adams office just before their closing time. The bookkeeper, her assistant, and the stenographer were on their way out. Adams told the secretary to run along as well. He'd take care of the locking up himself. With the women gone, he was ready to give Inspector Schmidt his full attention.

"You have news for me, Inspector?" he said.

"Did you know that you're one of the executors of your partner's will?" Schmitty asked.

"Yes. He told me. It was embarrassing because I just couldn't return the compliment. Tommy had no head for business, but Tommy relieved me of any embarrassment right away. He told me not to make him an executor of my will because he would refuse to serve. 'You know me,' he said. 'I'd just foul it up.'"

I knew Tommy Thomas. "Foul" is not the word he would have used, but that was only a detail. The meaning was there.

"That'll be a fat executor's fee," Schmitty remarked.

"I'll be waiving it," Adams said. Shrugging, he added, "In my tax situation, better the foundation have the spending of it than those apes in Washington and Albany and City Hall. I'm on the board of the Thomas Foundation and I flatter myself that we make better use of the money than any government—federal, state, or city."

Schmitty grinned.

"There are people who would tell you that's not hard to do," he said.

Adams laughed.

"I understand, Inspector. You are in no position to say it, since you are on the payroll."

The inspector laughed with him.

"On the other hand, the man who paid all that overtime to get those invitations faked in a hurry—I wouldn't say he was very smart about using money, would you?"

"Tommy? He never made any claims to being smart

about money. He used to come to board meetings and he'd sit and yawn and then go along on what the rest of us decided. If it came to a deadlock where he found himself having to cast the deciding vote, he'd just put his vote alongside mine. He had confidence in me."

"But he didn't consult you about spending such an excessive amount for those invitations?"

"Did he pay an excessive amount? I don't know. He'd never have consulted me about an expenditure like that. That was just pocket money. I was talking about real money, six-figure sums and more."

"In my league," Schmitty said, "there's no money that isn't real money, but that's not what I came to talk to you about."

"I was hoping not," Adams said.

"That old typewriter, Mr. Adams. It's the critical bit of evidence. Everything hangs on it and I want to be sure I'm completely straight about the facts concerning it before I go arresting anybody."

"I wish you wouldn't involve me, Inspector," Adams pleaded. "Friendships, loyalties."

"I won't be asking you to finger anybody," the inspector promised. "We'll talk about nothing but the typewriter. You don't have to sweat any about your loyalties."

Asking Adams to interrupt him and set him right if he should go astray on any detail, the inspector went back over that day when the machine had been left on the receptionist's desk with the instructions to the cleaning women for its removal.

"You work a short day in this office," the inspector said.

"We get better performance in less time, Inspector. That's what matters, not counting hours."

Schmitty wasn't interested in that.

"At what time does the night watchman come on and set up his book in the lobby where people who have business here after hours sign in and sign out, and at what time does the building open up to normal traffic in the morning?"

"You can ask about that downstairs, Inspector. It's something I wouldn't know. I also give better performance in shorter hours. I've never been in the office either that late or that early."

"I'd say, with your office schedule as it is, there'd be a couple of hours at the beginning of the day and another couple at the end of the afternoon when the building is open and you can come in and out without signing any book or even being noticed by anyone in the crowd."

Adams sighed.

"Yes, Inspector. Either that evening or the next morning Tommy could have come back to the office. I can't imagine that it would have mattered to him whether he had to sign a book downstairs or not. He was only retrieving his own property, he was doing nothing wrong. Afraid that I'd laugh at his sentimentality? Maybe that a bit, but he'd have no worry on that score. Even if he signed the book down in the lobby, I wouldn't know it. Also, it was more than sentimentality. He had a heavy touch on the typewriter. He just couldn't adjust to the action of an electric machine."

"You wouldn't know he signed the book," the inspector said, "unless we came to investigate."

"You can't think that he would have foreseen that, Inspector."

"No, Mr. Adams, but I would have expected that *you* would have foreseen the possibility."

"No more than Tommy, Inspector—less, in fact, since I knew nothing of his coming back."

"Yes," the inspector agreed. "That's so. He retrieved the typewriter and laboriously, working hours and hours on that wreck of a machine, he typed threatening letters to his last wife. Where would you say he put in all those hours of hard labor?"

"At home, of course. Certainly not here."

"Which home would that be, Mr. Adams?"

"He had only the one place. He'd turned the apartment over to Allegra as part of the divorce settlement. He was back in the carriage house."

"Where he had a cleaning woman who was into everything. Lottie Smith never saw a typewriter."

"Cleaning women!" The words were a sneer. "They always claim to be far more thorough than they are. Where else could it have been?"

"Since you ask, Mr. Adams, in *your* home. Have you replaced it there with Allegra's gun, or do you keep the gun on you?"

After that, Inspector Schmidt did all the talking. Adams just picked up his phone and called his lawyer. He didn't have to be informed of his right to remain silent. He knew it and he exercised it. So Schmitty talked and Schmitty told him what he was refusing to say.

Knowing Allegra and the big Texan act she liked to put on, Adams had planned his murder. All the evidence was to point to Allegra. The first step had been to persuade Tommy to dump the old typewriter. Adams needed that because it was so solidly identified with Tommy. He'd had a close call on that one: if the stenographer had found it worth taking home to her kid brother, he would have lost it, but it remained on the desk and it was no problem to return while the building was still open and sneak it out of there.

It was long hours' work typing the letters on that old wreck. Adams could never have managed it with the machine in the office unless he brought himself into the time when he would have to sign himself out of the building after hours. Allegra had not reacted quickly enough to the letters, and then, when Dodo's invitation arrived, he knew he had something with which he could concoct an outrage that would bring on an explosion. It worked as he'd hoped it would.

Allegra told everyone she was going to kill Tommy. Perhaps he had even hoped she might do his work for him, but he recognized that she was just talking. He was going to have to act for himself. She brandished her gun; stealing it out of her purse was easy. The rest was also easy.

He went home, picked up the old typewriter, the surplus faked invitations, and the cut-off pieces of letterhead, put them in his car, and drove to the carriage house. There he let himself in with his key and hid himself, waiting for Tommy to come home.

The inspector reminded him of the time when Tommy lost or mislaid his keys. They hadn't been lost or mislaid. Adams had taken them to have Tommy's house key duplicated. It had probably put him out when Tommy reacted by insisting on giving up his office key, since Tommy was going to have to have it if it was to seem that Tommy removed the typewriter from the receptionist's desk.

If that had ever seemed an obstacle, Adams had found his way around it. When Tommy came home, Adams let him go upstairs and undress before he revealed himself. Either Tommy came down for something Adams had known he would want out of the living room, or Adams made a noise that brought Tommy down to investigate. Either way, Adams was waiting for him and shot him in the back. Then all that remained to do was nip down to his car and bring the typewriter and the papers up to put them on the bedside cabinet on display.

While he was up there, he emptied Tommy's pockets of all the cash Tommy was always carrying.

"What was the point of that?" I asked. "In his tax situation and all the evidence he was stacking against Allegra."

"It wasn't money he'd report on his tax return," Schmitty said, riding along with my gag. He shifted back to his reconstruction. "He wasn't out to hang Allegra," the inspector said, "just out to kill Thomas and get away with it. He was giving us the largest number of false trails to follow—all six wives, a burglar."

"Why didn't he lock the door after him when he left?" I asked.

"That was probably part of his burglar picture."

"Careless Tommy failed to lock his door?"

"Either that or frightened burglar who has been forced to kill leaves in haste. By the way, he took care of the office-key problem by putting it on Thomas's key ring while he was into Thomas's pockets."

"But why?" I asked. "It can't be because Tommy as a partner was also 'guaranteed to fade.' They had gone on together for a long time, through all the marriages and before the first marriage."

"The reason why you held out on me," Schmitty said. "I still don't know."

"It all fits," the inspector said. "He came and went under Euclid's watchful eye, and Euclid was no time at all in locating him to come at him with his blackmail demand. He was someone Euclid knew, and Euclid knew where to reach him."

"That was idiotic," I said. "How could he not have realized that he would be seen and by someone who knew him?"

"It was stupid of him to think he had Euclid under control. He thought he had Euclid in his pocket."

"How?"

"Thomas had never gone for a married woman before, and all you people who knew him assumed he never would, but this time he did and that's why this time he did everything differently. No love tapes. You don't send those to your lady's husband's house. You break your life-long rule of never bringing a woman to the carriage house. You can't meet in her husband's house and you have to meet somewhere. Husband has his suspicions and he hires Euclid, who's admirably placed for it, to watch comings and goings and report."

All through this Vernon Adams had been sitting there in stony silence, listening to us and waiting for his lawyer. Now he moved. He pulled his desk drawer open and reached into it. I saw him come up out of it with Allegra's gun in his hand. Schmitty was on him before he could squeeze the trigger. He was raising the gun to his temple when Schmitty grabbed it and wrestled it away from him.

It was later, after Adams had seen his lawyer and he'd been taken in and booked, that I got the rest of it out of the inspector.

"You mean Marian Adams? Tommy broke up their marriage?"

"That's right, partner and oldest friend, but what's the difference? It was only a marriage, and in Thomas's book a man could always have another."

"But," I said, "that makes it even stupider for Adams to have put himself into Euclid's hands."

"I don't know. He didn't expect the kid to be expensive."

"Anybody would know that clamming up about a murder would command a price."

"The experienced businessman dealing with the barefoot boy. Euclid had that 4-H look. That was enough to fool Adams about him."

I wondered whether I had been stupid in never having thought of Tommy and Marian Adams, but I wasn't alone. No one who knew him thought of it. Dodo put it for all of us.

"How could we?" she said. "It was a real transformation. He was reaching the age where there could be no more virgins, not without some degree of cradle robbing. What none of us realized was that Tommy wouldn't do that. He had to adopt a new style, going for wives. It was either that or widows or old maids or divorcees. The old maids wouldn't have been to his taste, and divorcees had been through at least one failure. The poor lamb, he was looking for success. The one I can't understand is Vernon. Who would have thought he had that much passion in him?"

I explained that to her. I'd had it from the inspector. Tommy's murder hadn't been any crime of passion. Vernon Adams in his approach to killing had been practical. His wife had left him for Tommy Thomas. With Tommy out of the way, Vernon had expected she would be coming back to his hearth and home.